SWEET LOVE

JANUARY COVE BOOK 8

RACHEL HANNA

CHAPTER 1

She stood in the viewing room of the funeral home and greeted people for what seemed like days, but it was only a few hours. As the well-wishers passed by her, they hugged her and said things like, "Your mother was a good woman" or "Gone too soon".

In reality, she didn't hear much of it. They all sounded like the school teacher in the old Charlie Brown cartoons, a distant mumbling sound talking through a tin can.

Just get through this, she thought to herself.

Much of her last few years had been about just getting through things. She got through college. She got through her recently ended marriage. She got through her dull days at the job she hated. And now she had gotten through watching her mother suffer from breast cancer for the last two years.

Was this what life was like? A series of obstacles that one had to "get through"? And for what? What was the payoff? A nice long nap underground and entry into the pearly gates?

She wanted to go to heaven just like everyone else, but she wanted a grand adventure on Earth first. And this wasn't it.

Laura knew people meant well. No one knows what to say when a loved one dies. But right now all she wanted was to be at home, in her pajamas, sitting in front of the TV eating a pint of rocky road. And she wanted to wallow in her grief until her tear ducts ran dry. Mostly, she wanted to be left alone.

"Your mother was an amazing woman." The random woman hugged her as she moved through the never-ending line of mourners.

"Thank you," Laura said for the hundredth time in the last two hours. Her voice was starting to get hoarse.

The good part was that her mother had been well-loved, and rightly so. She had raised Laura alone for most of her life after Laura's father had died in the line of duty as a police officer. She had never remarried, but desperately wanted more kids so she took in foster kids for many years. One right after the other, a constant rotation of faces and stories and kids in need of love.

Laura had admired her mother for that, but her own childhood had often taken a backseat because of the needs of the kids. She wanted to say she understood and it was okay and be the bigger person, but a part of her resented it when she was younger. She'd wanted her mother all to herself, but maybe these kids needed her more.

"Your mother took me in when I was about eight years old. I think you were about six. Do you remember me?" the man asked. Laura nodded her head and plastered on a smile, but she had no idea who he was. Thankfully, he just hugged her and kept moving.

Was it possible to fall asleep standing up? She felt like it was. Her body was exhausted from the months of driving her mother back and forth to chemo, then weeks of standing beside her bed in hospice and this viewing was the last straw before her feet were finally going to give out.

There were times when she'd considered taking care of her dying mother a blessing. She was happy to be there because she adored her mother, but it didn't mean it hadn't been hard and tiring on her physically and mentally.

With no siblings to help out, the sole responsibility had fallen on Laura's shoulders. Her aunt Dahlia had been the only source of respite for her during the last few months. Dahlia had temporarily moved from her home in Oklahoma to the small suburb outside of Baltimore where her Laura's mother lived.

"How much longer is this?" her aunt whispered to her. She loved that about Dahlia - her ability to just cut right through the crap and say what she herself was thinking.

"Three years?" Laura whispered back, a fake smile still plastered on her face as people continued to pass.

The ironic thing was that her mother would have hated this whole idea of a viewing. She would've much preferred to be quietly sent off into heaven, her ashes scattered to the winds in her own front yard. She was just that way. A homebody. Not a person who enjoyed drama or fanfare.

But they hadn't discussed funeral plans. Ever. Her mother hadn't brought it up, and Laura wasn't willing to have that conversation. It was just too painful.

So Dahlia and Laura had settled on a viewing where they would receive friends and family, and then a small service with just the two of them scattering her ashes into the Atlantic Ocean.

"How are you two holding up?" Carrie asked. Laura had been best friends with Carrie for almost as long as she could remember. They'd met in fourth grade during a particularly challenging game of dodge ball at Sandy Ridge Elementary School. Laura, a petite and shy young girl back in those days, had been grateful for her then taller new friend's protection during the game.

Carrie had been raised with three brothers - Jake, Craig and Ryder. They were all so different from each other, but Laura had always been impressed with the love they had for each other. It was something Laura had missed out on, that love between siblings, but her relationship with Carrie had all but filled that void in many ways.

"I'm exhausted." It was all that Laura had to say before Carrie sprang into action.

"We want to thank everyone for coming tonight," she said to the small crowd gathered in the room. They were just standing around chatting now, no one else in line, sort of like people hogging a table at a restaurant while others are waiting to sit down. "The family would like to have some private time with Sarah now. I'm sure you all understand." She put on a sad smile and nodded her head as if trying to subliminally make them all agree with her. The thing was, it seemed to be working.

Within minutes, the room was cleared and Carrie was standing post at the door with her butt pressed against it to ward off any stragglers coming back in.

"Done," she said, clapping her hands together.

Dahlia laughed. "You're a hoot!"

Laura smiled at her friend and then gave her a grateful hug. It wasn't the first time her friend had saved her, and it probably wouldn't be the last.

Carrie was definitely the most outspoken of the two. In reality, it was amazing that they were even friends at all given Laura's shy personality. But something about their friendship just worked, and for that Laura was thankful.

"I hope they didn't think I was being rude…" Laura started.

"Oh, stop it. You have every right to need some down time, honey. People understand. And if they don't, well, screw 'em," Carrie said as she hugged her friend tightly. "Your mother wouldn't want you to get sick over this, and you know it."

Laura pulled back and wiped a stray tear from her eye. "I miss her already."

Dahlia crossed the room and hugged her niece. "I do too. I think we always will. She really did leave us way too soon."

Something about hearing her aunt say those words made them more real. Sarah had only been fifty-eight years old, yet cancer had swooped in and taken her down so quickly. Laura had never felt more helpless in her life than during her mother's treatments.

She'd had a partner in life with her mother. They were two peas in a pod; both shy and quiet with tough outer shells. Sarah had rarely dated, at least not around Laura when she was younger. Laura was much the same, having had only one real relationship in the last few years and that was with her now ex-husband. The one who didn't even bother to show up at the viewing. The one who promised they would stay friends no matter what and then ran off with a twenty-two year old flight attendant he'd met on one of his many business trips.

"I just want to go home, slide into a hot bath and listen to my classical playlist," Laura said, closing her eyes and taking a deep breath.

"Come on. I'll drive you home," Carrie said, sliding her arm around her friend and pulling her close.

"Before you go… Can I talk to you for a moment, Laura?" Dahlia asked, obviously uncomfortable about something. Carrie nodded and slipped out to give the two women privacy.

"What's wrong?" Laura asked, immediately on high alert. She couldn't take much more bad news.

"Nothing's wrong, sweetie," Dahlia assured her. "I just don't know how to say this. I can't help you go through Sarah's house. I just… can't…"

Dahlia started to break down, tears streaming down her cheeks. Laura had rarely seen her tough old bird of an aunt cry, so this was unusual. Dahlia was more of a free spirit, wearing her long flowing skirts and keeping her black hair in a bun on top of her head. A "flower child" right down to her name, Dahlia had adored her little sister with every fiber of her being. Although they were five years apart in age, they were extremely close.

"I don't understand… I thought we were going to go through it all together before we sell the house?"

Dahlia crossed the room and sat down in a chair by the door. "I just don't think I could take it, Laura. Saying goodbye like that... Well, I just feel like I can't do it."

"We could wait..."

Dahlia looked her in the eyes. "I just can't. I'm so sorry. I know this puts a lot of pressure on you."

Laura knelt down in front of her aunt and smiled sadly. "It's okay. I understand. I'll get Carrie to help me, okay? Don't worry about it. And I'll put some things aside that I know she would want you to have."

Her aunt reached out and hugged her. "Your mother was so proud of you, Laura."

"Thanks for saying that. I needed to hear it today." Laura stood and walked to her mother's casket, looking down at her lifeless body. It didn't look like her.

The funeral director entered the room, said a few things to Dahlia and then began the process of removing the casket from the room. Her body would be cremated soon.

As the two women stood in the empty room, Laura felt like her life was starting over, but not in a good way. She felt out of sorts and without direction. Spending so much time caring for her mother, she didn't know what she would devote her time to now.

"I think I should tell you that I'm moving back

home in a few days," Dahlia said quickly. She wasn't making eye contact.

Laura reached out and took her hands. "You did what you needed to do here. I would never expect you to keep your life on hold. Mom wouldn't want that. So you should go home. Tend to your gardens. Raise your mean llamas..."

"Oh, hush now! They aren't mean!"

They *were* mean. But they were Dahlia's babies, and it was time for her to go home and live her life.

Sadly, Laura had no idea what kind of life she was going to live. Nothing seemed to fit anymore. She felt adrift, and for the first time in her life, she had no idea what tomorrow would hold.

"SCHUSTER AND SUTTON. This is Laura. How can I help you?"

Laura was so tired of saying that same phrase over and over. Although she was an executive assistant, somehow her boss had let the receptionist go six months ago and never rehired anyone. So here she was answering the phones and doing her own job for the same pay... without complaining or standing up for herself.

It was all too familiar to her.

Her marriage had been much the same. Never standing up for herself and what she wanted in life, and when she finally did, he found another woman who wasn't so "mouthy" as he called it.

"Laura, did you reschedule my three o'clock?" her boss asked, poking his head around the corner of his glass enclosed fancy office. Mr. Sutton wasn't a bad guy, but he demanded perfection from all of his employees, and Laura was no exception.

"Yes, sir, I did. And I called Callahan about your meeting next week. I also put the file for the new fragrance client on your desk."

Working at a marketing firm had been interesting at first. New people, new products, good pay. But here she was almost seven years later with a salary that was close to the same when she started and the same cast of characters calling her phone everyday.

Dull.

That was her life.

She was now an orphaned, divorced, dull single woman with a small yappy dog named Rigoletto.

Ugh. Even she was tired of hearing her own sad, whiny voice inside her head. How had her life ended up this way?

At one point, she'd had this big promising future in front of her, and now she just felt like she could pack a bag and leave it all behind. Except her dog. She actually liked him.

When she'd met Ted, he was an up and coming architect with big plans to build big buildings in every major city. Life stretched out in front of her and seemed like an exciting adventure.

They'd both been in college at the time at the University of Maryland, although Ted was a year older than her. On the day of her graduation, he proposed and they married four months later. She loved the whirlwind, the not knowing where life might take her.

But life had quickly ground to a halt. Right after their wedding and short honeymoon to Florida, Ted had been offered his dream job right there in Baltimore.

Strike one - no big adventures.

Then, they learned that Ted would be traveling a lot... without Laura.

Strike two - Ted gets adventures, Laura gets loneliness.

The money had been good, no doubt, but it sure didn't keep her warm at night. And as the years went on and she settled into her own job, Ted's star continued to rise while hers seemed to drop into the ocean and settle to the bottom.

She felt left behind. While she cared for her mother, Ted traveled to Los Angeles and Vegas and even London. He met cool people and spent more time away from home. Away from her. Away from Dullsville, USA.

Although she was embarrassed to admit it to herself, she'd even asked Ted to have a baby with her at one point, mainly to give her something to focus on. When he declined, it should've been her first tip off that something was wrong. It should have been strike three.

But then her mother got sick, and all of her attention went to taking care of her. For awhile, she became obsessed with natural treatment options, even some that were out of the country, but her mother didn't want to go that route.

Everything came to a head one day about eight months ago. Knee deep in caring for her mother, Ted had come home from a business trip to Paris. He had this look on his face as he asked Laura to sit with him on the deck for awhile.

She sat calmly, digging her nails into the palm of her hand, while he explained that he'd fallen in love at first sight with a woman thirteen years younger than him, a flight attendant on his jaunt to Paris.

Her name was Chantal, and she was apparently everything he ever wanted. Fun. Spontaneous. Perky. Romantic.

All of the things Laura had wanted to be for him before he basically abandoned her for his job.

She hadn't even argued with him. At the time, she was exhausted already, both physically and emotionally, so she just took a deep breath and let him go. Honestly, she thought he'd come back, but he never did.

Social media pictures showed a very different

man. Committed. Fun. Adventurous. The man she'd dreamed of having was now giving all of that to another woman.

"You ready to go?" Laura was suddenly tugged back out of her repetitive daydream as Carrie arrived at the office.

"Huh?"

"Lunch? You do still eat lunch, right?" Carrie smiled broadly as if coaxing her best friend into the world of happiness again.

"Oh, yeah. Sorry. I was just..."

"Reliving history, as usual?"

Carrie knew her better than she knew herself.

CHAPTER 2

The two women sat at a small bistro table outside of their favorite restaurant. Carrie was digging into her enormous salad while Laura picked at her club sandwich.

"What is going on with you today?" Carrie finally asked, staring at her friend with her fork hanging in midair.

"Nothing. I'm fine." Laura took in a deep breath and sighed.

"Oh really? You don't sound fine. You sound like your lungs are collapsing. Come on, Laura. I've known you our whole lives, so don't try to play me."

Laura stared at her for a moment and smiled. "Okay. I'm not fine. I'm bored."

"Bored? How is that possible when you live this life of constant adventure?" Carrie said sarcastically.

"Of course you're bored, Laura. You never take any risks."

"Um, excuse me?"

"What was the last risk you took?"

Laura could hear the theme song to Final Jeopardy playing in her head.

"Talking to you on the playground in the fourth grade."

Carrie giggled. "Probably true. But listen, maybe your life is calling to you to take a risk. Do something crazy. Move out of your incredibly boring comfort zone."

"And how am I supposed to do that? Everyone and every thing I know is right here in Baltimore."

"Laura, don't take this the wrong way, but everyone is living their lives and you're stuck."

Laura's stomach clenched. She knew Carrie was right about that, but she had absolutely no idea what to do about it.

Carrie reached her hand across the table and grasped Laura's. "Nothing is holding you here, sweetie. You did your part and took such great care of your mother, but she'd want you to move on with your life. It's been a couple of weeks already, and you haven't even begun to go through her house, honey."

"I'm just not ready yet…"

"I don't think you're ever going to be ready to say your final goodbye to her, but I'll help you. Okay? Let me help you get moving in the right direction."

Laura smiled sadly. "Are you trying to get rid of me?"

"Of course not! Besides, I'll probably just follow you wherever you go anyway. There are hot men all over this fine country of ours!" she said, putting her hand over her heart like she was about to sing the national anthem.

"And you aim to date all of them, right?"

"It's my patriotic duty," Carrie said with a wink.

IT WAS a weird sensation to be in her mother's house without her. Even the sound of the beeping machines and random medical alarms would be a welcome distraction right now, she thought as she shut the door behind her.

Gone was the adjustable hospital bed that had been in the middle of the living room for so many weeks. Now there was just this big empty space that reminded her yet again that her mother was gone.

Laura stood there for a moment and took it all in, determined to start going through her mother's things today so that she could take at least a small step forward in her own life.

There was a lot to go through given that her mother was a "saver". She was somewhere between a collector and an outright hoarder, but definitely leaned more toward hoarding while still being clean and fairly organized.

She walked into the kitchen first, figuring it would be the easiest place to start. The first half hour was spent simply tossing everything in the refrigerator into the trash and then hauling it out to the street for pickup.

Laura was keenly aware that she was stalling. The last thing she really wanted to do was go through her mother's personal possessions alone. In all reality, she'd expected Dahlia to stick around and help her, but she couldn't blame her aunt for feeling overwhelmed by the thought. She certainly felt that way right now.

"Yoo hoo, anybody in here?" she heard Carrie call from the front entryway.

"Back here. In the kitchen," Laura called, thankful to hear her friend's perpetually chipper voice.

Carrie rounded the corner carrying two big brown grocery bags and a smile on her face.

"Mongolian beef and sesame chicken from Szechuan Village, plus a big bottle of your favorite wine. I'm ready to help!"

Laura laughed. Leave it to Carrie to make a sad "cleaning out my dead mother's house" event more of a party.

"I'm starving. I totally forgot to bring food, and cleaning out Mom's fridge did little to entice me.

Have you ever seen lasagna that is way past its prime? Not a pretty picture. Or smell."

"Yeah, I think I still smell it. You got any air freshener around here?" Carrie asked as she put the bags on the counter and started rummaging through the cabinets like she lived there. She'd been raised just around the corner, so Carrie knew every square inch of the house, probably as well as Laura knew it.

After wolfing down copious amounts of Chinese food and a couple of glasses of wine, the two women started sorting through the living room together.

"Magazines?" Carrie called from behind the sofa.

"Recycle."

"Cross stitch patterns?"

"Donate." Funny thing was that her mother had no clue how to cross stitch. She had no clue why she would have had the patterns in the first place.

"Human head?"

"What?" Laura said as she jumped to her feet and stared at Carrie wide-eyed.

"Just making sure you were paying attention."

Laura's heart was pounding. "Totally not funny."

"It was a little bit funny," Carrie said as both of them broke into a real-life case of the giggles.

The next hour was spent sorting through the rest of the living room, and Laura was surprised that things were going at such a rapid clip. Of course, she hadn't dared to go into her mother's bedroom yet because that was where the memories really were.

Family picture albums. Keepsakes. The smell of her mother's perfume.

"I think we've about got this room done. You ready to tackle the next one?" Carrie asked, apparently undaunted and full of energy even though it was almost nine o'clock at night.

"I think I'll probably call it a night..." Laura started to say. She wasn't tired. She was procrastinating, and Carrie knew it.

"Are you sure you aren't just putting off dealing with your mother's bedroom?"

"What are you, a mind reader?"

Carrie walked to her friend and pulled her into a hug. "I'm here tonight. Why don't you let me help you with her room? She was like a mother to me too."

Laura pulled back and looked at her. "I think it's something I need to do alone. I hope you understand."

"Of course I do, sweetie. I'm a phone call away if you need me, though. And I'll bring ice cream next time."

Laura smiled. Ice cream had long been "their thing". Rocky road had been there when crushes didn't return their affection in middle school. Mint chocolate chip had been the answer to many a heartbreak in high school. And butter pecan had gotten Laura through her divorce.

After Carrie left, Laura stood there in the middle

of the living room for a moment, taking in the ever-dwindling nature of her mother's house. It seemed smaller now that her presence was no longer there.

She made her way down the hall to the first door on the right and pushed it open slowly. The creak that desperately needed oiling sounded so much louder now.

After flipping on the overhead light, she caught a glimpse of the work ahead and sighed.

"Oh, Mom, why did you keep so much stuff?" she said softly through a sad smile before the first tears made their way down her cheeks.

"Look, man, I did everything I could. They just aren't interested in renewing."

Sawyer Griffin paced the floor of the small office, refusing to look at his agent - otherwise known as the bearer of bad news.

"I've been with them for five years, Dan. I don't understand the hesitation," he said, slamming his fist down on the desk. Dan jumped a bit and cleared his throat.

"Settle down, Sawyer. I've never seen you this upset."

Sawyer took a deep breath and ran his hands through his thick sandy blond hair before sinking down into the fake leather chair in front of Dan's desk.

"I released three amazing albums. Fans loved them. And now the label is dropping me?"

"The last album was…"

"A departure. Yeah, I get it. But I was tired of singing those damn cookie-cutter songs. I wanted to be the artist that I really am."

"Well, those cookie-cutter songs are what the fans love, man. You gotta please the fans."

Sawyer stared out the small window over the Nashville skyline. "No, I don't. I can't do that anymore."

"So what are you saying?" Dan asked, crossing his arms as he leaned back.

"I'm saying I'm… done. With this."

"So that's it? You're just giving up your career?" Dan's eyes were wide. "You can't be serious."

Sawyer took a breath and then nodded. "Yep. I'm going home." He stood and walked to the door.

"Home? What the heck are you talking about?" Dan asked as he jumped up and followed him. "Where is home?"

Sawyer smiled like he knew some secret. He stopped and turned to Dan. "January Cove."

❧

THE SUNLIGHT PEEKED through the window blinds and right into Laura's cracked open eyelids. She turned away from the blinding light and remembered where she was - her mother's bedroom.

Somewhere during the hours and hours of sorting and packing, she'd apparently crawled up into her mother's bed and fallen asleep. The sheets smelled like her mother, and they were a welcome comfort right now.

Funny how grief takes a vacation during sleep, but the first moment a person opens their eyes in the morning it's back to the real world. And sometimes reality sucked.

The sound of Laura's cell phone beeping finished waking her up as the light of the screen brightened the room even more. She slid across the bed on her belly, reaching her arm to the nightstand, and looked at the screen. There were four messages from Carrie, all at different times.

1:15AM: How's it going?

2:54AM: Everything okay, sweetie?

6:17AM: Okay, what's going on? You need to answer me!

6:53AM: I'm at your front door. I'll give you five minutes to respond before I kick it down. And you know I can do it!

Laura looked at the time. It was 6:57. She quickly ran to the front door and opened it just in time to see Carrie running toward it, obviously part of her attempt to kick it open.

"Stop!"

Startled, Carrie grabbed her chest. Laura rubbed her eyes in the morning sun.

"Why didn't you answer me?" Carrie asked, obviously filled with worry.

"I was doing this thing we call *sleep*…"

"Yeah, well, don't do it again," Carrie grumbled as she picked up a white paper bag from the porch railing and walked past Laura into the house. "I brought breakfast."

"Why are you here so early?" Laura asked as she closed the door behind them.

"Because I know you need help getting this place finished up so you can get it on the market."

Laura was really spoiled having such an amazing, loyal friend, and she knew it.

"Do you ever sleep?"

"Waste of time," Carrie said smiling as she pulled two huge blueberry muffins out of the sack. "Muffin?"

"Sure," Laura said, catching it in mid air after Carrie tossed it. She was sort of impressed with her catching skills.

"How far did you get in your mom's bedroom?"

"Well, I went through her closet. Got a lot to donate there. She definitely wasn't a fashionista, God rest her soul."

Carrie smiled. "Remember that awful yellow and brown flowery dress she used to wear to your school events?"

Laura giggled and stood up. When she returned from the bedroom, she had that very dress in hand. "She kept it! Can you believe that?"

"Can I please have it?" Carrie asked, a serious look on her face. "I mean if you don't want it?"

"Want it? I was going to burn it. I don't even feel right donating this thing!"

"Then can I have it?"

"You're serious?"

"Of course. It's a great memory from my childhood, watching your mother waltz into school looking like a nineteen-seventies sofa."

The two of them had a good laugh, and Laura gladly gave Carrie the dress. It was true that Carrie had loved her mother almost as much as she had. The two of them spent just about every day together as kids, either at Laura's house or Carrie's.

"So, what else did you go through?"

"I went through all of her drawers, the big wooden chest, her bathroom cabinets..."

They walked down the hall into her mother's room. Carrie looked impressed at that progress Laura had made.

"I'm really surprised you got so much done without me... or ice cream," she said with a laugh.

"Ice cream would've given me a sugar rush and

then a crash... much like this bag of candy did," Laura admitted, holding up a huge bag of mini candy bars that she'd munched on until she was about to pop in the wee hours of the morning.

"Seriously? You bad woman, you. I thought you were on low carb?" Carrie teased.

"Shhh.... The carbs can hear you, and you might hurt their feelings..."

"Okay, toss me a Snickers and tell me what you're going to do about that," Carrie said, pointing to the mound of stuff sticking out from under her mother's bed.

Laura threw a Snickers bar at her, barely missing her nose. She was never great at sports, which was evidenced in her getting kicked off of two softball teams in her life.

"Well, I may have been procrastinating on that."

"Nah... really?"

"How did you know I wouldn't get to that?" Laura asked with a smile.

"Because I know you better than you know yourself. And I know that your mother kept all of her prized possessions under there, for whatever crazy reason."

Laura sighed. "It was easier going through her clothes."

"Come on. We can do this together. And you can call the real estate agent tomorrow and get this house on the market."

"Why the rush?"

"It's been weeks, Laura. You know you're stalled on this, and I'm going to un-stall you."

Laura finally relented, knowing that her best friend wasn't going to give up anyway. They sat down on the floor next to the bed and began the task of digging everything out.

"What on Earth is this?" Carrie asked as she pulled out some long pink pieces of shiny ribbon.

Laura smiled. "Oh, I remember those! Mom was a ballerina in high school. These are her pointe shoes."

"Wow. I didn't know she danced."

"Yeah, she loved it, but her parents couldn't pay for lessons anymore when Grandpa had his accident."

Laura's late grandfather had been in a farming accident when her mother was in high school, and his inability to work had really put a strain on the family.

"Oh, wow... Look at this," Laura said as she slid a large picture frame from under the bed. "It's her high school diploma. And here's her college degree too," she said. Her mother had graduated with an associates degree as a legal secretary, and that's how she had supported Laura all those years alone.

They spent the next hour laughing over the memories they pulled out from under her bed, and

Laura was surprised that the task wasn't as bad as she'd feared it would be, at least not with Carrie.

"Have you seen this?" Carrie asked, her eyes wide as she looked at a large piece of white poster board that she pulled from under the dusty bed. "Here, take a look."

She handed it to Laura. The poster board was yellowing and the corners were turning up, but clear as day at the top was written "My Dream Board".

"I think it's like her vision board or something," Carrie said, scooting in closer, craning her head over Laura's right shoulder. There were pictures taped to the paper along with big words written across it.

"My mom didn't even know what a vision board was," Laura laughed.

"Well, apparently she did because we're currently looking at it. Look, she wanted to ride a roller coaster and sky dive..."

"She was terrified of heights, just like me!"

"And it says she wanted to go on a date... with a younger man? Go, Sarah! She was a cougar!"

Laura scowled. "My mother was not a cougar."

"Look, there's even a picture of a motorcycle here..."

"This doesn't make any sense!" Laura said as she shook her head. "My mother wasn't this person. She didn't want to date younger men and ride motorcycles. She liked quiet evenings on the front porch, sipping lemonade and listening to crickets chirp."

"And maybe the occasional hot younger man…"

"Carrie, that isn't funny."

"Why are you getting so bent out of shape about this? So your mom had dreams you didn't know about."

"She would've told me!"

"Oh really? Do you honestly think Sarah would've told you about this stuff given how straight laced you are?"

Laura's mouth dropped open. "Straight laced? What is that supposed to mean?"

Carrie smiled sadly. "Honey, you have to admit that you're not exactly a daredevil. Maybe your mom had this other side to her that she wanted to express but she was afraid of what people… you… might think. And maybe this vision board is really old, from when you were little, and she couldn't run off and do these things."

Laura considered what her friend was saying. Maybe her mother had felt constrained by her life, just like she was feeling right now. And then her time to do something about it had run out.

"Look at this one," Carrie said, pointing to a small postcard taped to the bottom left corner. It was a beautiful beach with an aqua blue ocean.

"What did she write there?" Laura asked, leaning in and squinting her eyes.

"It says 'my dream home.'"

"Is that the Bahamas or something?"

Carrie studied the picture for a moment. "No. It says 'January Cove, Georgia'. Did she ever mention that place?"

"No. Never. Not to me at least." Laura was starting to feel like her mother had this secret life she knew nothing about. Why wouldn't she share her dreams with her only daughter?

"So what are you going to do about this?" Carrie asked as she sat back against the bed frame.

"What do you mean?"

"Well, your mother never got to achieve these dreams, and you need a fresh start so..."

"Oh I get it. I'm supposed to run off with a younger man on a motorcycle and see if he'll take me skydiving?"

Carrie laughed. "Sounds like the perfect date to me."

Laura stood up and tossed the poster board on the bed. "Well, not to me. I'm not going to run around and live my mother's dream board."

Carrie stood up and crossed her arms. "When are you going to jump out there and do something crazy, Laura?"

"Carrie, you can't be serious about this. I have a life here. I have a *job* here."

"That you hate," Carrie said as she followed her to the kitchen. Laura poured a glass of orange juice and leaned against the kitchen counter.

"Well, it's still a job."

Carrie sighed. "What do you really want out of life?"

"I have no idea," Laura said softly before setting her glass on the counter.

"Exactly. Now is the perfect time to explore what you really want in your life. Nothing is holding you here. You're getting a nice check from your mother's life insurance, plus this house will sell quickly and you get all the proceeds. You could live anywhere and do anything! Doesn't that excite you?"

"No. It terrifies me, actually."

Carrie smiled. "Good. Life should be a little terrifying when we're making big leaps."

"Your clients must pay you the big bucks for this advice," Laura said with a laugh. Carrie had been a life coach for about three years, working with people on the Internet from all over the world.

"Yes, they do, actually. But they listen to me, and you don't."

"I am listening."

"No. You're arguing. How about this - let me make your big life decisions for the next three months, and we'll see what you think at the end of that time."

"Have you lost your mind? I'm not letting you make my decisions for me, Carrie. I'm a grown woman!"

"Fine. But at least promise me that you'll give this some thought, okay? Nothing is holding you here, sweetie. You've got all of the options in the world right now, and most people would kill for this opportunity. I'm just saying that living out some of your mother's dreams might help you get the peace you want and start your own life over too. And maybe you'll come up with some dreams of your own in the process."

Laura smiled and sighed, thankful that her friend was giving up the argument... for now anyway.

CHAPTER 3

Sawyer stood at the end of the pier and
stared out over the familiar coastline. He'd
spent his entire life smelling that salty sea air, and it
was a welcome scent to him now that he was back
home.

So far he'd managed to fly under the radar, but
he'd only been home for a few days. At some point,
someone from his past would definitely see....

"Sawyer?" he heard a voice say behind him.

He turned around to see another familiar sight -
Brad Parker, one of his oldest friends and constant
running buddy from high school. Although they
hadn't seen each other in years, Brad's smile was the
same as ever. A prankster at heart, they'd gotten in
trouble many times together over those turbulent
adolescent years.

"Brad! Wow, you look old, man!" Sawyer teased. Brad stepped forward as if he was going to hug him, but instead pushed him a bit to make it appear as if he was going to plunge directly into the waiting ocean below. Sawyer braced for the fall just as Brad grabbed him with his other hand and hoisted him back up the pier.

"Did you learn nothing about making fun of me?" Brad said with a laugh before he finally pulled Sawyer into a bear hug. "What are you doing here, dude? Shouldn't you be singing at the Grand Ole Opry or something?"

"Ha ha ha… Very funny. Just taking some much needed time off."

"Well, you know you're going to get mobbed by adoring old lady fans here, right? You're the talk of the town. The big celebrity that makes January Cove proud. The hometown son who…"

"Alright already!" Sawyer said, putting his hand over Brad's still moving mouth. "I can see not much has changed. You've still got a big mouth and flabby abs."

"We don't all get to work with celebrity trainers," Brad said, rubbing his barely visible stomach. Since he started dating Ronni a few months ago, she'd gotten him into yoga - one of her "California" activities that she brought with her down South. "So why are you really back in town?"

"I told you. I'm taking a break." Sawyer turned

back to the water and stared out at the tiny dots out in the ocean that must have been boats.

"You could take a break anywhere. I saw your last break in People magazine. Aruba, right?"

"What are you? Some kind of stalker?" Sawyer asked with a chuckle.

"I just wanted to be able to say I knew you when."

"When what?" he asked, turning around.

"When we TP'd City Hall. When you fell into the ocean right about there trying to get away from that yellow jacket that you *thought* was chasing you." Brad added air quotes for effect. "When we dated those sisters from Savannah. Remember them? One is a nun now, I heard. Kind of a weird twist of fate, huh?"

"Do you ever stop talking?" Sawyer knew the answer to that. Brad was funny, curious and a bigger gossip than any woman he'd ever met. But he had to admit he loved the guy like a brother.

"Now I think you know the answer to that," Brad said as he leaned against one of the posts of the pier.

"So, what's new in your life?"

"Well, I'm still a contractor. Just finished the renovations on the old Lamont theater."

"Yeah, I saw that place. January Cove is stepping up in the world, huh?"

Brad smiled. "I'm pretty proud of how that turned out. My girlfriend runs the place for a development company out of California."

"Girlfriend, huh? You mean a woman finally took you under her wing out of pity?"

Brad chucked his friend in the arm. "I've missed having you around, buddy. What do you say we have dinner tonight? There's a great restaurant called Breakers…"

Sawyer sighed and looked at Brad. "I'd love to catch up, but I don't want the attention right now. Kind of looking to get away, if you know what I mean."

"Gotcha. I forgot you're a celebrity. To me you're just a pimply faced teenager with only a passing acquaintance with deodorant and a terrible curve ball."

Sawyer laughed genuinely. "It's good to be home." It truly was good to be home where his real friends didn't think of him as famous or anything special. He was just Sawyer from January Cove High School. "Raincheck on dinner?"

"Sure. Listen, Addison owns a B&B so why don't we set up a time for dinner sometime soon? That way the gawkers won't hassle you trying to take selfies or whatever."

Sawyer smiled. "I'd love to see Addison and the rest of the crew if possible. Give me a few more days to settle in, and we'll do it. I'm staying in the yellow rental house off Elm for at least the next few weeks."

Brad nodded and shook Sawyer's hand before he headed back up the pier. Yes, it was good to be back home, but for the first time in his life Sawyer felt like a tiny little boat adrift in the wide open ocean - without direction or a plan. In reality, he had no idea where he even wanted to go in his life. He could feel a door closing, but another one didn't seem to be opening.

~

LAURA GRIPPED the phone tightly in her hand as she stared out the small window diagonally across from her desk. To be so close to downtown Baltimore, her view sucked. She felt cooped up, like she was in prison.

"Mr. Dennon, I've explained in every way I know how that we didn't approve that marketing campaign. Your wife is the one who gave the final go-ahead on that..."

The older man continued interrupting, as he usually did in their weekly phone calls. His mind was faltering, and he blamed Schuster & Sutton for any errors with his company's marketing even though they usually originated with him or his awful wife. Yet, Laura had been instructed not to irritate one of their biggest clients. No. Matter. What.

She just needed to sit there and take it, according to her boss. Mr. Sutton would play off the fact that the client was always right and force Laura to just nod and smile, but it was starting to drive her batty.

When the old man finally finished his long diatribe, she hung up the phone and put her head in her hands. She'd literally had the same headache for a couple of weeks now.

Laura stood up and stretched her back as she walked to the window and looked out. Everything in her view was gray and dreary, including the sky today. She was so tired of living the same life every-day. Get up, go to work, go home, cook for herself, entertain herself. Boring, that's what it was. Her soul was dying.

"Laura, did you handle Mr. Dennon's issue?" her boss asked from behind her.

"Of course I did. I always do." She added that last part, and the bitterness in her voice was hard to mistake.

"Excuse me?"

She turned slowly, realizing what she'd done. Mr. Sutton had very hard edges, and right now she could see the irritation on his face clearly. But for some reason, she didn't care.

Maybe it was because her mother's insurance check was on its way. Or maybe it was because the Realtor had called this morning with an offer from a buyer before the sign even went in the yard.

"I said I always do," she repeated. "I have the same conversation with Mr. Dennon every single month when he forgets he or his wife signed off on the billing for a marketing campaign."

He glared at her as if he couldn't believe she was standing up for herself. "Well, that *is* your job."

Mr. Sutton started to turn to walk out, but Laura spoke before he could. "No. Actually, it *isn't* my job to listen to someone berate me for half an hour for something I didn't do. My job here was supposed to lead me to becoming a marketing executive, Mr. Sutton. But instead I find myself caught in a position with no future potential, and I haven't had a raise in four years!"

Now her voice was traveling ever higher, and she couldn't seem to control it. The last thing she wanted to do was be seen as an over-dramatic woman.

"Laura, after all of our years together, I can't believe how you're talking to me right now. I'm very disappointed. I realize you've been... emotional... lately, what with your mother's death and your husband leaving you..."

His tone was that of a father disciplining a child, and it made her start to feel rage seething under the surface. How could she have missed it? He saw her as a child? Beneath him? It was as clear as day to her right now.

"I quit."

The words escaped her mouth before she even had time to consider what she was saying, and for a moment she wanted to suck them right back in like a Hoover vacuum.

"What?" His eyes were wide and his jaw slack as his mouth hung open. "Are you kidding me?"

Laura took in a deep breath, fully aware that she was standing at a fork in the road. She could either stay in her comfortable, boring rut or she could make a break. Try something new. Be the person she actually wanted to be instead of the person everyone expected her to be.

"No, Mr. Sutton, I'm not kidding," she said calmly. Evenly. Peacefully. "I quit."

Without another word, she turned and opened her drawer, pulling her handbag from it. She picked up her favorite candle from her desk and a picture of her chihuahua, Rigoletto, and stuffed them into her bag. Mr. Sutton continued staring at her as if the power of speech had left his body.

"I want to thank you for employing me all of these years. Really. It was mostly a pleasure. I wish you well, sir," she said as she walked past him and out into the lobby. As she stepped on the elevator, she could see him still standing in the hallway.

Looking down at her phone, she sent a quick text to Carrie.

Quit my freaking job. What now, life coach?

CARRIE TOOK a long sip of her wine as the early spring breeze swept across the table of the small cafe. Laura sat there, expectantly waiting on her friend to direct her, being the successful life coach that she was, but instead Carrie continued staring at the screen of her small laptop.

"Hello? Unemployed middle aged woman looking for direction here," Laura said, waving her hand around as if she was in distress.

Carrie tilted her eyes up at her friend and smiled wryly. "Yeah, I get it. I'm actually doing a little research here."

Laura slid her chair around and craned her neck toward the screen. "What's that?"

"That, my friend, is a tourism site about January Cove."

"What? Why are you looking at that? I thought you were going to help me with my joblessness problem. Instead you're staring at pictures of the ocean?"

Carrie sighed. "Can you even think outside of the box for just a moment? This is your chance to break away from this place that you find so dreary right now and start something for yourself. The cost of living and starting a business in January Cove would be minuscule compared to here. Plus, you have just about year-round tourism opportunities there."

"Starting a business? Who said I was starting a business?"

"Why wouldn't you, Laura? You'll have a nice

financial nest egg once the house closes. It could be life-changing."

"Or I could put it into a high yield account and retire a few years earlier..."

"Boring." Carrie said, fake snoring. "Why don't we just move you right into the assisted living center over on Dagwood Avenue? Jeez, Laura, this isn't like you."

"What isn't like me?"

Carrie closed her laptop and reached across the table, taking her friend's hands in hers. "Don't take this the wrong way, but Ted really screwed you up, sweetie. You started changing from this bubbly, albeit introverted, girl into this stuffy, unbending woman when you met him."

"Thanks a lot," Laura said, pulling her hands back.

"You used to have dreams. Remember?"

Laura reached back in the back recesses of her mind, and she was slightly surprised at how far back she had to reach. She felt like a little girl on her tiptoes trying to reach something on the highest of shelves.

"We all have dreams when we're young, Carrie. And then we grow up."

"No. I don't accept that. You are only limited by your mind, Laura. I've seen it time and time again with my clients. You hold the keys to your kingdom, and it's simply a shift in your thinking that will open the whole world to you. You can either decide that this is it, and this place is all you'll ever have. Or you can decide that childhood dreams are worth pursuing, and you can pursue yours at the same time that you honor some of your mother's unrealized dreams."

She knew Carrie had a point, although she hated to admit it. A smile creeped across her face at the thought of her biggest dream.

"I remember when I was about fifteen, you and I wrote out our biggest dreams. Do you remember?" Laura asked.

"Of course. I thought I'd marry Brad Pitt and we would own an island near Fiji. Do you know he still hasn't called me?" Carrie huffed with fake indignation.

"Do you remember mine?"

Carrie thought for a moment. "I do. You wanted to open a bakery, right?"

Laura felt her heart warm up in her chest when she thought about it. That had been a big dream for her for so many years, but she'd pushed it away. She had even asked Ted to back her financially a couple of years into their marriage so that she could start a bakery, but he refused, giving her a bunch of reasons that made little sense to her. It basically boiled down to the fact that he didn't believe in her.

"Do you think I could really do it?" she asked,

hopefulness seeping into her voice and scaring the crap out of her at the same time.

Carrie reached back across the table and took her hands. "I know for a fact you could do it. And what better place than this little January Cove town? After all, that would mean I can come visit the beach any time I want!"

At first Laura smiled, but then it left her face. "We've never been apart, Carrie. I need you."

"Oh, honey, I need you too. But I love you too much to watch you die here. You have so much to give, Laura. And you deserve a new start. I just don't think it can be here. You know that saying that if you love something, set it free? That's what I'm trying to do here."

Laura sucked in a deep a breath. Was she really going to do this?

SAWYER SAT at the kitchen table at Addy's Inn and watched his old friend, Addison Parker, chase her one-year old daughter around the kitchen. The child was a "rounder", as his great aunt would've called her, toddling around the kitchen and getting into everything she could reach.

"Anna Grace, no, sweetie…" Addison chided as she pulled the little girl's hands away from the tall plastic trashcan behind the counter. "Sorry, Sawyer. I'm listening." She picked Anna Grace up and put her inside of a play area surrounded by plastic gates that made it look more like a prison inspired at Toys 'R' Us.

"Oh, I was just saying that my contract was up and we mutually decided not to renew. I wanted some time to just decompress, ya know? I mean it's been years since I came home."

Addison sat back down in the chair across from him and sighed, wiping her bangs out of her eyes. She was still the little girl he remembered, irritating her older brothers and their friends. But those Parker kids had always been tight, and now that she was married to Clay - who was like a another Parker brother - she seemed so grown up.

"Well, I'm glad you came home. I know Brad was pretty excited when he told me last week. He needs a running buddy. Of course, he's pretty smitten with Ronni these days."

"I know. I can't believe a woman finally decided to keep him," Sawyer said with a laugh. "How's your mom?"

"Oh, she's good. You know Adele Parker. Always on the move with her new husband, Harrison. He's a good man, and he takes care of her. Well, I guess they take care of each other. She'll probably be back soon because Jenna is due any day! You remember Jenna, right?"

Sawyer chuckled. "Of course. Kyle and Jenna

were the ultimate high school power couple. I mean they were older than me, but I remember them dating. And breaking up. It was all the gossip back in those days. I need to make time to see Kyle while I'm here."

"How long will you be here?" she asked, brushing some stray Cheerio crumbs into a pile on the edge of the table.

"Probably a few weeks at least. I mean until I figure out my next move with my career. Lots of good opportunities..." he said, drifting off and hoping she didn't hear how much of a liar he was. The truth was that he had no opportunities. No one had called. His last album had been a flop, making him doubt his own abilities as an artist. After all, people only liked his music when it fit the mold. When he ventured outside of the "norm" and did the music he loved, his fans dispersed like a stink bomb had gone off.

"Well, good. That means you can come to the JCHS reunion!"

Sawyer swallowed a lump in his throat. "Um, a reunion?"

"Yes, silly! Of course you have to come. It's for several classes because it wouldn't make sense to have a reunion for one small class at a time. Brad will be there, and probably Kyle and me too. It's going to be down on the beach, near the ferry dock

45

in a few weeks. Big bon fire, food, music. Everyone is bringing their families too."

The last thing Sawyer wanted to do was go to a reunion right now. Why couldn't it have been a couple of years ago when he was in his heyday and killing it in his career? How was he going to explain why he wasn't living the dream in Nashville right now?

"Oh. Good. Just let me know when you have more details."

"Well, I hate to rush off, but I have a brand new visitor coming to stay here today. I've got to get a room ready. Do you mind seeing yourself out?"

"No, of course not. Thanks for the coffee and cookies," he said as he stood up and gave Addison a quick hug. "You have a beautiful place here, Addy. I'm proud of you."

"Aw, thanks, Sawyer. I'm proud of you too, Mr. Bigtime Country Music Singer." His stomach clenched.

Addison picked up Anna Grace and walked upstairs. As he heard her footsteps going down the long hallway, he made his way to the front door, pausing for a moment to look at the Parker family pictures in the hallway.

There was Adele, the matriarch of the family. She never changed and looked much like she did when they were in high school. Then there was a big family picture including a couple of women that Sawyer didn't recognize.

He smiled when he thought back to those old days of playing in the surf and chasing every pretty girl around JCHS. He'd been one of the big men on campus, so to speak, never hard up for date. Invited to every party. But his home life hadn't been such a bed of roses.

His mother had died when he was a toddler of some rare cancer that he tried not to think about. His father had been a bit of a womanizer even when his mother was alive, and it didn't take him long to marry another woman. A younger woman with fake blond hair and poorly done fake boobs to match.

By the time Sawyer entered high school, his father had been married two more times and had decided to move out to Arizona with the newest one. Her name was Barbie and she lived up to the name.

Sawyer ended up staying with his great aunt in January Cove while his Dad went and sowed his wild oats. It had been years since he'd seen his father, although he got several letters from him when he released his first album. Typical - show up when it suited him so he could brag about his son's newfound fame.

As he looked at the Parker family photos, he smiled at the memories he'd had with January Cove's resident family. When his own father had let him down, they took him in and treated him like one of their own.

Jolted out of his walk down memory lane by the sound of Addison soothing her daughter upstairs, Sawyer quietly walked out onto the porch and closed the door behind him.

It was late afternoon, and he could smell the salty sea air even though the B&B was across the street from the beach. The constant breeze in January Cove made for moderate temperatures almost year round.

He stared up at the blue sky. There wasn't a cloud anywhere to be seen. Truth be told, he'd missed his childhood home and the people who had known him long before he was "something". Now he had no idea who or what he was.

He walked to the end of the cobblestone walkway leading to the B&B and onto the sidewalk. Across the street, he could see a new business going in but he couldn't quite make out what it was going to be. He secretly hoped it was a good burger joint, but that was unlikely given the number of restaurants scattered all over town already.

As he stepped down onto the deserted streets of his small hometown, he looked to the left and recalled fond memories of his youth. Visions of the JCHS Homecoming parade danced in his head. He could vividly remember riding on the huge float with his baseball teammates and throwing candy to the little kids standing on the sidelines. To them, he was a hero. A baseball standout. A musical prodigy.

Now he had no idea who he was. Somehow he'd veered way off his course of wanting to be a serious music artist. Instead he'd ended up as a country music star singing someone else's songs and not using his gifts. He felt hollow and shallow and detached.

He closed his eyes and took in one more deep, salty breath before he felt it...

CHAPTER 4

*L*aura had been driving for more hours than she cared to count. Instead of stopping over in some rural town she didn't know, she'd decided to drive straight through which was almost ten hours if she didn't have to pee, which was unlikely.

Her friends had always kidded her that her bladder was the size of a Barbie doll's, and it was getting worse as she got older. One sip of water, and she was sure to have to stop ten times to get rid of it. It was one of the mysteries of her life.

She pulled into January Cove and felt a smile forming on her face. It really was a quaint little town, and she could see why her mother was attracted to it. She wondered if her mother had ever been there, or did she see it in some random magazine? These were questions she would probably never get answers to.

Before she'd left town, she sent a letter to Dahlia telling her she was going to do some traveling for awhile and would text her occasionally. Dahlia wasn't one to pry, and she didn't want anyone showing up in January Cove until she got settled there, so the details she gave were few.

Of course, Carrie knew exactly where she was and Laura was sure she'd pop up at some point. Carrie was spontaneous that way.

As she pulled down the main road, she felt at home already. No taxi cabs everywhere. No police sirens. No big, tall buildings blocking the sun. This place was a cozy little corner of a busy world, and she hoped it might heal her and bring her back to life.

She would be staying at a place called Addy's Inn, evidently run by someone named Addy? As she looked down at the GPS on her phone quickly, she felt a bump and then heard a scream before she slammed on the breaks in her tiny compact car.

"Oh my God. Oh my God. Please be a squirrel..." she said to herself as she opened the door of her car. Logically, she knew it couldn't be a squirrel because of the strength of the thud, but hope reigns supreme. Instead, what she saw shook her to the core. A man was lying on the ground, writhing in pain, holding his right leg.

51

Otherwise, he looked okay. He was moving. He was breathing. And he was yelling.

"What the hell, woman? Are you crazy?" he yelled, anger and pain contorting his face. It was a nice face. She wondered briefly what it would look like with a smile.

"I'm so sorry. I was a bit lost and I…" she said as she knelt down beside him and tried to figure out what to do to help him.

"You were looking at your phone? Owwww…." He was in a lot of pain, so she decided it was better not to argue with him right now.

"Let me call 911," she said. "Crap. Where's my phone?"

"Oh the irony," he mumbled under his breath.

She turned around and noticed the sign for Addy's Inn. "Oh, would you look at that. I wasn't lost after all." The man shot her a glare that could've killed her. "Right. 911. Let me…"

"Oh my God! Sawyer? Are you okay?" a woman asked as she ran out of the inn. It was probably his wife. All the good looking men were taken.

"I accidentally hit him with my car. I was about to call 911…" Laura stammered, tired from her drive and mentally exhausted from… life.

"Here. Use my phone," the woman said, pulling her phone from her pocket. She teetered a little girl on one hip while she knelt down and started checking the man over. Sawyer, apparently.

Laura quickly dialed 911 and waited while the woman ran back into the inn looking for supplies to help treat the cuts and scrapes that had started to appear. The man couldn't sit up and held onto his leg, but he wasn't speaking to her or making eye contact.

"I'm Addison, by the way," the woman said as she reappeared.

"I'm Laura. I'm... your new guest. If you'll still have me. I'm so sorry. I didn't mean to hit your husband."

Addison smiled. "He's not my husband. We grew up together. Don't you recognize..."

The blaring sirens broke the peacefulness of the small town as the ambulance appeared from a side street. Two men jumped out of the front, and another popped out of the double doors on the back.

"Sawyer? Dude, you don't look so good," one of the guys said jokingly.

"Funny," Sawyer replied, his face wincing as he tried to move.

"Damn. I'm sorry, man. I didn't realize it was so bad," the guy said as he knelt beside him. "We're going to stabilize you and get you to the hospital ASAP, okay?"

Within minutes, they strapped him to a gurney and lifted him into the ambulance, speeding off just as the sun was starting to make its descent.

Laura stood there, her car still parked in the middle of the road, unsure of what to do.

"I'm sure he'll be okay," Addison said softly. Her daughter toddled around in the front garden as she kept a watchful eye on her.

"I should've stopped for a rest. I thought I was lost. I looked at GPS and then..."

"Come on. Let's get your car properly parked and then we can get you settled in." Addison put her hand on Laura's back to urge her toward making some kind of move. "I'm sure the police will want to talk with you."

The police. Laura's stomach churned as she thought of the fact that she'd only been in town a few minutes and was already needing to be interviewed by the local police.

After an hour she had, in fact, been interviewed by the police. They made the determination that the whole thing was an accident for now, but charges could still be brought later after they interviewed Sawyer. She was instructed not to leave town.

As she settled into her room, she felt wave after wave of guilt wash over her. Was he okay? Did he break any bones? She paced back and forth as she thought about this stranger she'd injured until she couldn't stand it anymore.

"Excuse me, Addison," she said as she peeked into the kitchen. Addison was feeding her daughter a late dinner. A handsome man was also in the kitchen and smiled at her as she entered.

"Oh, hi, Laura. This is Clay."

"Nice to meet you," she said with a forced smile. "Listen, can you tell me how to get to the hospital? I feel so bad…"

"Sure. Let me draw you a quick map," Addison said, handing off the feeding duties to Clay.

Laura drove down the dark, mostly deserted roads of January Cove. She could see why the man had been standing in the middle of one because it was a small town, mostly quiet. She wondered what tourist season was like since summer was about to begin soon.

She pulled into the hospital parking lot and walked through the ER entrance. There was one nurse behind the counter and a bunch of empty chairs lining the walls of the waiting area.

"Hi. I'm looking for… what's his name… Sawyer?" She felt like a complete imbecile, not even knowing his last name. The woman smiled graciously.

"Honey, I can't just let you back. Especially not with Sawyer being back there."

That comment made no sense to her, but she was focused on getting back there. "I'm the one who hit him with my car."

The woman's mouth dropped open. "You hit him

with your car? Why? He's such a nice guy. And super hot!"

Laura sucked in a sharp breath and struggled not to lose her cool with the young woman behind the desk. She was tired from her drive and emotionally drained from worrying about the handsome stranger she'd accidentally mowed down with her car.

"Look, I realize he seems to be somewhat of a local celebrity but..."

"Seriously? He..."

"Can I help you?" There was a man standing off to the right of the front desk who'd been listening to part of their exchange.

"Well, I'm not sure," Laura said. "Unfortunately, I'm the one who hit the gentleman with my car."

She was so embarrassed. Everyone had looked at her like she'd pushed the Pope off a cliff or something.

"I'm Brad Parker," the man said with a genuine smile.

"Any relation to Addison?"

Brad smiled again. "Yep. She's my sister."

"Nice to meet you," Laura said as they stepped a few feet away from the front desk. "I'm Laura Bennett."

"Sawyer is one of my oldest friends."

"Oh. I'm so sorry. How bad is it? It was an accident. I looked at my GPS for a second..."

56

Brad chuckled. "I once pushed him off a roof when we were thirteen. He's fairly tough even though I tell him he's a wuss most of the time."

Laura's anxiety lessened a bit as she finally took in a real breath for the first time in hours, it seemed. "So he's okay?"

"Why don't you come on back and see for yourself?" Brad said.

"But I'm not family."

"Neither am I, Miss Bennett.," he said with a wink. Jeez, were all the men in January Cove so good-looking? She thought for a split second about Carrie and how she would walk around this town with her tongue hanging out if she were there.

Laura followed Brad through the double doors as the girl behind the front desk gave her some serious "side eye". The hospital wasn't state of the art by any means. It was a bit old-fashioned with big cream colored tiles on the floor and wood paneling on the lower half of the walls. But somehow it felt comfortable and safe, unlike the hospitals she'd been in with her mother for so many months. They felt cold and lonely no matter how many people were around.

They turned left at the small nurse's station, and Brad pushed open the cracked door to reveal the man lying in the bed, his leg elevated and in a brace of some kind. He had his eyes closed, but there was a scrape just above his right eye and his right arm was in a sling.

"Oh my God. I did that to him?" she whispered to Brad.

"He's going to be okay, Laura. The doctor said he'll be out of commission for a couple of weeks. He didn't break any bones, but it did some damage to one of the ligaments in his leg. The doc explained it, but all I know is he'll wear that brace for a few weeks and maybe do some rehab."

"And his arm?"

"Just a sprain. He'll be out of that in a few days, most likely."

Her face contorted as she looked at him. She felt horrible for the pain she'd caused him, and she kind of wanted to slink back out of town before everyone realized what an idiot she was.

"They gave him some pretty powerful pain pills, so he might be out for awhile. You're welcome to wait, if you'd like."

"Okay. Thank you."

Brad walked toward the door. "By the way, welcome to January Cove," he said with a chuckle before shutting the door behind him.

What a welcome it was.

IT WAS DARK. He could hear it coming. Was that a train? He could feel the reverberations of it on the ground beneath his feet, but he was stuck in quicksand. He pulled and tugged but couldn't release its grip on his feet. The sound was coming ever closer. He could feel it about to hit him and…

"Stop!" he screamed, waking himself up. A hand touched his arm, and then brushed across his forehead.

"It's okay," the female voice soothed. "You're okay…"

He struggled to open his eyes. Why was he so dang tired? His eyelids felt like they had lead weights on them, and his throat was dry as a bone. Where was he? And why did he feel tied down?

Finally, he willed one of his eyes to open. It was bright, wherever he was. He could hear a machine beeping somewhere off in the distance, and his leg was caught. When he tried to move it, pain ricocheted through his body like a ping pong ball.

"What the hell…" he mumbled, gritting his teeth through the pain. Then he heard a bit of commotion, a door opening, felt a warmth through his arm and then no more pain.

Was he dead?

He wasn't going out like this - a quitter? No thank you. He willed his other eye to open. Everything bright. Everything blurry.

"Where am I?" he managed to mumble. A figure came into view, although blurry. Female, he thought, but he couldn't tell much more.

"You're at the hospital, Sawyer. But you're going

to be fine, okay?" the woman said, again stroking her hand across his forearm. Even in his current state of confusion, it felt good. Her touch felt natural. She was a good nurse, whoever she was.

"Light. Too bright."

His eyes started to focus when she turned down the sun-like beacons above his head. He could see the shape he was in now. Leg elevated in a brace. Right arm in a sling. Nurses milling around on the other side of the window.

Turning his head, he saw her. The "her" who had put him in this predicament in the first place. That was a face he'd never forget.

"Who let you in here?" he demanded, his throat constricting from the dryness. She turned and filled a small cup with water and put it in his left hand.

"Brad let me in," she said softly. "I came to check on you. And apologize. I'm so very sorry for what happened."

He took a long sip of the water and wondered if this was what people lost in the desert would feel like having their first drink in a long time.

"Please leave," he said after downing the liquid and regaining most of his voice.

"Excuse me?"

"I don't want you here."

"But I wanted to apologize."

"And you did. Now please leave before I have to call security."

"Dude, calm down. Jeez," Brad said as he appeared in the doorway.

"Why did you let her in here?" Sawyer said, obviously angry at his friend. "I told you I wanted my privacy."

"Because she wanted to see how you were doing, man," Brad said, a hint of warning in his voice. "You're being rude."

"Are you freaking serious right now? She put me here!"

"Sawyer…"

"Excuse me. If you two don't mind, I'd like to get a word in here," Laura said. Both men stopped talking and looked at her incredulously. She moved to the side of Sawyer's bed. "Look, I made a terrible mistake today. I glanced down at my phone for a second and you were standing in the middle of the road. I didn't see you, and I caused these injuries. I'm very, very sorry. I will pay your medical bills, or you can file charges and send me off to your local jail if you'd like. But, I would also like to point out that you were *standing in the middle of the road*. I'm not from around here, but where I live people don't just stand in the middle of the road staring at the sky like that."

"So this is my fault? Is that what you're saying?" Sawyer asked through partially gritted teeth. The nerve of this woman!

"Yes. Partially, anyway. I take my part of the

responsibility, but I think you also have to take yours."

Brad struggled not to laugh, and the sight of it was irritating the crap out of Sawyer. He wanted to come up out of the bed and slug his friend, like he had many times in their youth, but his list of injuries was preventing that at the moment.

"You've said your piece. Now can you please leave?" Sawyer said softly without looking at her. If he was honest, he had a hard time looking at her. She was beautiful, but in that "girl next door" sort of way. Her long neck was distracting, and her emerald green eyes looked lost and alone.

Without a word, she gathered her purse from the chair and walked out the door. When Sawyer looked at Brad, he stood there with his arms crossed.

"What?"

"I know what you're thinking," Brad said with a sly smile.

"Oh really? And what is that, genius?"

"Why did the hottest new woman in town have to hit me with her car?"

Sawyer sighed. Brad knew him far too well.

Ma'am? The sign is ready to go up," another man

CHAPTER 5

o one was more surprised than Laura
when she got word that Sawyer wasn't
pressing charges against her. She hadn't seen him
since the hospital fiasco two nights before, but
Addison had told her that he was home now, at least.
Her plan was to stay as far away from him as possible, and maybe he would leave town before their
paths accidentally crossed again.

Her focus now had to be on her new business.
Hitting the hot guy with her car was but a minor
blip in her rearview mirror now, she thought, and
then felt bad for the pun.

"Where do you want this?" the man asked as he
wheeled in another refrigerated display unit. The
place was coming together, and she would be
opening in just a few days.

"Right over there. Against that wall," she said.

"Ma'am? The sign is ready to go up," another man said as he poked his head through the front door.

Many sleepless nights and phone calls with Carrie had finally led to the name of her new bakery - "Sweetcakes".

"Let me grab my phone so I can take a picture," Laura said, fully knowing she couldn't advertise her new business on social media without her aunt getting wind of it. She wanted to achieve some success before anyone close to her found out about her new venture.

As she watched the big sign go up on the side of the brick building, she couldn't help but feel some anxiety. This had been her dream for so many years, and now it was a reality. She owned a bakery. Her success - or failure - was in her own hands now.

But then she thought about how Ted hadn't believed in her, and that set a small fire inside of her belly. She wanted word of her successful bakery to get back to him one day.

"A bakery, huh?" Brad said as he met her on the sidewalk.

"Yep. Cupcakes mainly, although we'll do some special order cakes too. Opening this week," she said with a smile.

"Love the name."

"Thanks. Listen... how's Sawyer?" Why was she tugging at that string?

"He's better, but he needs help."

"Help?"

"Yeah. He doesn't start rehab just yet, and he's having some trouble taking care of himself. Cooking. Cleaning. That kind of thing."

"Surely he could hire an in-home nurse or something?"

"Too stubborn for that," Brad said with a laugh. "I just came from seeing him, actually. Took him twenty minutes to open a can of soup."

"Well, did you help him?" Laura asked, her hand on her hip.

"I tried, but the guy gave me attitude so I let him do it. Ended up with chicken and rice all over the table."

Laura felt her stomach churning. She caused this. The poor guy was sitting at his house, probably covered in soup.

"Listen, can you give me Sawyer's address? I'd like to have something delivered."

Brad smiled. "Of course." Why did she feel like he was up to something all the time?

After getting everything done at Sweetcakes for the day, Laura headed back to Addy's. When she walked inside, there was a buzzing of activity she hadn't seen before. Addison was running around, talking about an octave higher than normal. Clay was furiously packing things into a diaper bag.

"Everything okay?"

"Oh. Laura. Sorry. I didn't see you there,"

Addison said with a big grin on her face. "My sister in law is in active labor, so we're heading to the hospital."

"Jenna, right?" Laura was trying to remember all of the major players in the large Parker family, but there were quite a few of them.

"Yes. She's bringing my beautiful new nephew into the world before this day is over!"

"Oh, how exciting!" Laura said, trying to match Addison's elevated level of enthusiasm.

"I made a casserole and a salad, so it's in the fridge if you get hungry. I'm not sure if I'll be back for breakfast in the morning…"

"No worries, Addy. I can feed myself." Addison giggled.

"Okay. I just like to take care of my guests."

"You go. This is such a magical time for a family. Take all the time you need."

Moments later, Addison and Clay were out the door, along with their little girl, and Laura was left alone. She'd been so busy since arriving in January Cove that some alone time was certainly in order, but when she sat on the front porch to try to read her book, her mind was distracted. She couldn't stop thinking about Sawyer and his soup stained shirt.

"BREATHE, Jenna. Come on, honey, you gotta stop holding your breath, okay?" Kyle said as he held his wife's hand. Her forehead was sticky with sweat, and her face was red from the intense contractions. The doctor said they would be pushing sometime soon.

"I'm trying..." she mumbled between the tough contractions.

Jenna loved the Parker family, and she'd been a part of them for most of her life. But right now all she wanted was her husband, so everyone else was banished to the waiting room.

Adele Parker had arrived in town just in the nick of time. She and Harrison, her new husband, sat with all of the other Parkers as they nervously awaited the arrival of the newest family member - Mason James Parker.

Jenna had insisted they call him Mason, but Kyle was partial to "MJ". They would argue about that later, she had decided.

"Are you ready to start pushing, Jenna?" the nurse asked as she started preparing the area for a new arrival.

Jenna nodded and took a deep breath between the contractions. "I'm ready."

Kyle looked down at his wife, the love of his life and his high school sweetheart. "Then let's get ready to bring our son into this world."

LAURA SAT on the front porch of Addy's Inn and surveyed the main drag of January Cove. Only two cars had passed in the last hour, so she could see how Sawyer felt safe standing there in the middle of the road.

The place was quiet, with only the sound of her classical music playlist and ocean waves crashing in the background behind her new bakery. She couldn't wait to set up a few bistro tables on the back deck so that customers could stick around and watch the ocean rolling into shore while they enjoyed one of her homemade strawberry cream cupcakes. The thought made her smile as she closed her eyes and took in a deep breath of the salty sea air.

She was startled out of her pleasant thoughts by the sound of a man clearing his throat nearby. When she opened her eyes, she was shocked to see Sawyer standing there on his crutches, his lower leg in some kind of an air cast and his right arm still in a sling. How he had managed to balance on crutches with a sling on one arm was beyond her.

"Sawyer? I didn't see you there."

"Seriously. Maybe you need to get an eye exam. Or maybe I've got some kind of invisibility super power around you?"

She wanted to laugh at that, but he wasn't cracking a smile. For such a good looking man, he sure was serious.

"Here. Have a seat," she said, standing up and

pulling another rocking chair close by. Surprisingly, he didn't argue and eased himself down into the chair while Laura held it.

His brow was covered in sweat, and it was very apparent that he had struggled to get himself over to Addy's. It was almost nine o'clock at night, so she wasn't sure why he was even out of his house right now.

"It's awfully late for you to be out walking around on crutches, isn't it?"

He chuckled, mostly to himself. "Am I supposed to be a hermit now that you've maimed me?"

She opted to ignore his sarcastic comment. "Did you receive my delivery?" Proud that she'd sent a week's worth of dinners to his house from a local chef, she hoped that he would see that as an olive branch and a real apology for what she'd done.

"Yeah. That's why I'm here."

"You didn't have to come all the way here…"

"I don't need your charity."

Now she was getting irritated. "Excuse me?"

"I can take care of myself."

"Oh really? How was your soup today?"

He cocked his head at her. "How did you know about that?"

"I have my sources."

"Brad. I'm going to kill that guy."

Laura smiled, although he couldn't see her on the darkened porch. The light from the front door was just enough to illuminate his strong jawline and the stubble around it. And she could barely see the light shining through his ocean blue eyes that were framed by the most amazing black eyelashes she'd ever seen.

"He was just trying to help. And so was I." Sawyer said nothing. "Look, I know that I made a huge mistake. I was exhausted from driving way too long without a break. I was lost in this little town, as hard as that might be for you to believe. And I only glanced at my phone for a second. I just didn't see you standing there..."

"I shouldn't have been standing there."

He said it so softly that she barely heard it. "What?"

"You're right. A grown man with a brain should not stand in the middle of any road." She thought she saw a bit of a smile on his sexy face. Nice. "I came here to say thank you for the food and that I accept your apology for almost killing me."

Laura laughed. "I think that might be overstating it a bit. But thank you for not welcoming me to town by sending me to jail."

"What kind of music is this anyway?"

"Um, classical. Surely you've heard of it."

"I thought only old people and elevators played it, though."

"Nice," she said, rolling her eyes. Why didn't

people understand the beauty of classical music? "It's really all I listen to. It calms me."

"So is that your new business across the street?" he asked.

"Yes."

"Sweetcakes?"

"It's a bakery. Mainly cupcakes."

"Do I get free cupcakes since you almost took my life?" He craned his head toward her, an actual smile on his face. Dang it, he was bad news. That was a sexy smile. A sexy, country, Southern smile.

"Sure. Every time I almost kill you, I'll give you one free cupcake."

Sawyer laughed. "Where's everybody tonight?"

"Addy and Clay left a few hours ago. Apparently Jenna was in active labor, but I haven't heard an update since they left."

"Huh. Time sure passes quickly," he said, leaning his head back against the chair and staring out into space.

"It definitely does."

"I remember being a kid, running out in the streets. Playing ball. Being in parades. Riding my bike. And now Kyle and Jenna are married and having a baby. Crazy."

"Yes, I've been reminded recently that life is short."

Sawyer turned and looked back at her. "What happened?"

"I just lost my mother recently after a courageous battle with cancer. In fact, I'm only here because of her right now."

"I'm so sorry for your loss, Laura. And for being a jerk after our little accident."

"Oh, is that what we're calling it now? A little accident?" she asked with a smile.

"Well, I'll heal up soon enough. And you taught me the lesson of never standing in the middle of any road. All my big plans of standing in the middle of the interstate are now dashed, thanks to you." He smiled, and two dimples suddenly appeared. Yum. "So where are you from?"

"Baltimore."

"Ahh... Nice city. I've only been there once."

"What were you doing there?" she asked. He looked stunned at her question for a moment and then spoke, offering a small crooked smile.

"Oh, just passing through. You mentioned you were in January Cove because of your mother. What did you mean by that?"

Laura squinted her eyes. "You'll make fun of me." He used his good leg to lightly kick her chair.

"Come on. I won't laugh. I promise." He was already starting to smile. "Look at me. I have no room to laugh. You could easily push me out of this chair right now."

Laura giggled. "I came here to live out my mother's dream board."

"Dream board?"

"Well, I guess it's technically called a vision board."

"You lost me."

"When my mother died, I inherited her home. I found this big board under her bed, covered in years of dust. It showed all of these different things that she wanted to do in her life, but I know that she didn't get any of them done. So, here I am."

Sawyer laughed. "And January Cove was her big dream?"

"Hey, I already love this little town."

"Yeah, I guess it's a pretty cool place," he said.

"Anyway, January Cove was just one little picture on the board, so I started here."

"What kinds of other things were on the board?" He was leaning in closer, obviously interested in her strange tale.

"Just random stuff. This and that..."

"Out with it. Give me some examples." He sat waiting with a big smile like a Cheshire cat. It was the biggest smile she'd seen since hitting him with her car, and it was causing butterflies to rush around in her stomach.

"Roller coaster. Sky dive. Motorcycle. Date a younger man..." she rattled off as quickly as she could.

"Date a younger man?" Sawyer could barely contain his laughter.

"Hey! There's nothing wrong with a woman dating a younger man!"

"Didn't say there was. Sorry. I just wasn't expecting that." He cleared his throat nervously.

Laura smiled. "Yeah. Me either. My mother was a demure, conservative woman. I can't imagine her wanting to do any of these things."

"So why are you doing them then?" He leaned back in the creaky rocking chair and adjusted his arm, wincing a bit.

"I guess I just realized that life is short, and a person should follow their dreams while they can." Laura leaned back in her chair and sighed, trying not to get emotional when she thought about her mother.

After a few moments of watching her, Sawyer finally spoke. "Can I ask you something?"

"Sure."

"What about your dreams?"

Laura cocked her head to the side quizzically. "What about them?"

"Well, do you have dreams?"

"Doesn't everybody?" she asked with a laugh.

"I'm not sure they do. Or maybe most people think that their dreams are way out of reach."

"One of my dreams is in process, right there across the street," she said, pointing to the new sign on her bakery.

"Good. Everyone should follow their dreams. You only get one shot at this life."

"What about you? Are you following your dreams?"

He fidgeted a bit in his seat and laughed nervously. "I have been for a long time." He said it softly and then changed the subject before she could dig further. "Listen, can I ask you a favor?"

"Depends on what kind of favor. If it's a 'can I borrow a dollar' favor, then sure. If it's 'can I borrow a kidney' then I'll need more time to think about it."

Sawyer chuckled. "But you wouldn't immediately say no to a kidney loan? That's progress right there, my friend." Laura smiled, and there were those butterflies again. "Actually, I was going to ask if you minded helping me out a bit tomorrow?"

"With...?"

"My physical therapist called a few hours ago. Apparently I need to be there tomorrow just before lunch for my first session. They want to start working on my arm so I can get back to..."

"Work?"

"Something like that. I was wondering if you could maybe... drive me there? If you're busy with the bakery, I totally understand. I can ask Addy or even take an Uber... if we have Uber around here..."

Laura reached across and touched his arm without thinking. "It's okay. I don't mind at all. I sort of owe you that much, right?" He looked down at her hand resting on his tanned skin, and she immediately pulled back.

"Good. I really appreciate it. My house is right down there. Just take a left at the stop sign, and it's the third one on the left. A small yellow cottage with a red mailbox." As he pointed, she tried to pay attention, but his jawline was particularly distracting to her for some reason.

"Got it. Red mailbox." Lord, she hoped she could remember what he just said. As she was contemplating having him repeat it, he somehow managed to stand up on his own, reaching for the crutches that were leaning against the porch post.

"Here. Let me help you..." She retrieved both crutches and slipped one under each arm, although with a sling it wasn't easy. "How are you getting home?"

"I'll take the moron home," she heard Brad say from the sidewalk.

"Moron?" Sawyer said.

"Dude, do you not remember I was coming by tonight? Bringing wings and beer?" Brad held up a bag that had grease bleeding through onto the brown paper. "Got a little held up at the maternity ward."

"Do they even still call it that?" Laura asked under her breath.

"I do," Brad said with a wink. "Come on, man. I'll take you home and give you a sponge bath."

Sawyer grunted and looked at Laura. "About ten tomorrow?" She nodded and smiled.

"Ten it is. Red mailbox." Sawyer eyed her carefully for a moment, lingering longer than she expected before Brad cleared his throat.

"Addy and Clay should be along anytime now. They were right behind me," Brad said to Laura.

"So the baby was born?"

"Yes, a beautiful baby boy. Mason James Parker. Carrying on the handsome male lineage of this family," he said, flexing the muscles in his arms.

"Dear Lord, come on, you goober," Sawyer said, poking his crutch out at Brad and knocking his shin. "See ya tomorrow."

As Laura watched them get into Brad's truck and drive down the road, she felt something she hadn't felt in a long time. And that was enough to scare the crap out of her.

CHAPTER 6

"**W**ait, so you ran over a guy with your car?" Carrie said from the other end of the phone line.

"I didn't run him over. I just tapped him. Hard." Laura held her cell phone on her shoulder with one ear while she poured a cup of coffee. Addison had gone back to the hospital to see the baby and Jenna while Clay went to work at the ferry dock, his side job that seemed to be more for fun and socializing than any real need for money.

"And he's still speaking to you? And he's hot?"

"I never said he was hot."

"You never said he wasn't. I know you, Laura."

Laura sat down on the bar stool and stirred the cream and sugar into her coffee. "And what is that supposed to mean?"

"You have the hots for this guy!"

"Why on Earth would you say that?" Laura's cheeks flushed hot, and she could only imagine what color they were at the moment.

"Because you've told me precious little about your new business or the town or anything else except this guy."

"I just started from the beginning." Carrie could always tell when she was lying.

"Mhmmm…."

"Anyway, I have to go soon because I need to scarf down this blueberry muffin and coffee and pick him up for physical therapy."

"I bet you'd like to give him some *physical* therapy!" she said, giggling like a middle schooler.

"Goodbye, Carrie," Laura sang back to her, laughing as she ended the call.

ADDISON SMILED at her new nephew. He was adorable, for sure. He had a tuft of dark hair on top of his head which almost looked a little bit like a really bad toupee. The thought made Addison giggle to herself.

Addison was truly happy for Jenna and Kyle. There had been many years that they had been separated, but Addison was so glad that Jenna was officially her sister. And now that they had their first child together, it really solidified their family unit.

With Jenna's little girl, Kaitlyn, from her previous marriage, Kyle finally had the perfect little family that he so deserved.

"She's so beautiful," Addison said to her brother who was packing Jenna's bag to go home.

"Handsome. He's handsome, not beautiful." Kyle smiled at his sister and continued packing.

"Whatever. He's going to break a lot of hearts one day."

"As long as no one breaks his heart," Jenna said with a giggle. And Addison knew that was true. Her sister-in-law would do anything to protect her children, so little Mason had no idea what his mother might do to future girlfriends if they broke his heart.

"So did I hear correctly that Sawyer Griffin is back in town?" Kyle asked.

"Yes. But I feel like he's hiding from something. He says he just needs a break from the limelight, but I get the feeling that something happened back in Nashville."

"Maybe so. But if he needs to get away, we all know January Cove is the perfect place for that," Kyle said.

As Laura drove down the street, she looked carefully for the red mailbox. She thought to herself that she should've paid better attention when

Sawyer was talking, but she had had a very hard time focusing. When he smiled and was nice to her, he was extremely appealing and that fact alone was quite distressing to her.

She turned on the road and started counting houses, thinking that she remembered that his house was the third one on the left. It seemed that she might be right when she spotted the red mailbox.

It was an adorable little yellow house with a wraparound front porch, somewhat bigger than the other small beach homes in the area. She didn't know if he owned it or was just renting it for a short time, although she thought someone had told her that he was only back in town temporarily.

If nothing else, she didn't need to be getting interested in someone who was only staying for a short time anyway. She planned to lay down roots in January Cove, and getting involved with someone who wasn't planning on staying was not in her future plans.

In the back of her mind, she could hear Carrie's voice telling her that life was short and she should jump out there and just be happy. Even if that happiness was only for a short time.

"What am I thinking? This guy isn't interested in me any more than I'm interested in him." Even though she was trying to convince herself of that, she found herself feeling interested in him. Maybe it was just the long drought of not being with someone who really cared about her. It had been a very long time since a man had loved her; since a man had touched her in a way that made her feel cherished and safe.

Maybe she had hit her head when she knocked him to the ground with her car. Whatever the reason, she'd have to be careful not to let her feelings get out of hand.

She pulled into the driveway and parked her car. As usual, she was early, a pet peeve that had driven her ex crazy.

"Why do we have to be everywhere fifteen minutes early?" he would complain every single time they had to go to a family function or a party.

She didn't know why, other than her mother had taught her that being punctual was basically an unwritten rule, and being early was even better.

"Good morning," Sawyer said as he opened the door. He still had that morning look of tousled hair and he wasn't yet wearing a shirt, something she tried hard to ignore but couldn't.

Dang, he was good looking. The stubble along his jawline had grown overnight, and his chest was chiseled like he'd been carved out of stone. No matter how hard she tried, it was impossible not to notice the thick, deep crevices on both hips that led down to places she would rather not think about.

For a moment, she felt like she was having a hot

flash, but she wasn't in that time of her life yet. *Please don't let my cheeks be red.*

"Sorry I'm a little early..." she said as she walked inside. The place was clean as a whistle and had beach furniture, as expected. It was light and bright and not at all what she expected.

"No problem. I need a little help anyhow," he said. Laura turned around to face him again, trying to get her bearings and tamp down her hormones.

"Help?"

"Today hasn't been a great day. I tried to pull on my shirt and I think I further injured my arm." She could see a mint green t-shirt slung over the chair beside them. "I don't suppose you could help me get that on?" He squinted his eyes and forced a smile.

"Of course. That's no big deal. Here, let's get this thing off first..." she said, reaching out to help him remove the sling. He winced a bit as she did it, obviously in pain. "Have you asked for some pain meds?"

"Nah, I'll be alright in time," he said, his deep Southern drawl causing heat waves throughout her body. As she removed the sling, she noticed a well worn guitar in the corner.

"You play?" she asked, pointing to it. Anything to distract her from the feel of his warm skin against her fingertips.

He looked at the guitar and then cocked his head at her, looking a bit confused. "Yeah."

"You any good?" she asked, smiling as she took the shirt from the back of the chair.

"A lot of people seem to think so."

"Well, if I help you with this shirt, you have to promise to play me a song once you're out of this sling. Deal?"

"Deal. I'll even sing too."

"Are you a good singer?"

He laughed. "I can carry a tune." It was like he had some kind of inside joke that she didn't understand, and not wanting to look stupid, she didn't dig further.

"Well, good. I can't wait to critique you." She pulled the hole down around his head, her fingers grazing the edge of his stubble. She wanted to linger there, to feel if it was prickly or soft, but thought better of it.

He carefully lifted his hurt arm into the shirt first, his hand catching along the way. For a moment, all she could hear was her breathing, deep and ragged, and his seemed to match. Probably from the pain of lifting his arm, she convinced herself.

"Critique me?" he said softly as she held the shirt out for his other arm. She could feel his breath across her cheek, and it was blowing a stray strand of her hair slightly.

"I love music."

"What kind?" he asked, as she finally finished pulling his shirt down. Over rock solid abs, her fingers purposely grazing the crevices of each indentation in hopes that he didn't notice.

"I told you last night. Classical."

She couldn't be sure, but it sounded like he grunted.

"Not a fan?" she asked with a laugh.

"Never really got into that," he said, as she helped him put the sling back on. "You like country?"

"Yuck. No thanks. Nothing but songs about heartbreak and people dying."

"But elevator music is better? Classical sounds like music you'd hear at the grocery store. Or in a funeral parlor."

She furrowed her eyebrows at him. "Don't tick off your driver, Sawyer."

He smiled. "Fine. We can table this discussion for now."

After a few moments, they made their way out the door. Laura helped Sawyer into her small car.

"Where to?" she asked.

"Just take Main Street down past the ferry dock and go right. The therapy office is a few miles from there."

At first they rode in silence, and Laura wasn't sure what to say. Small talk had never been her strong suit.

"Cats or dogs?" Sawyer suddenly asked.

"What?"

"Do you like cats or dogs?"

"Dogs. In fact, I have a little doggie. He's currently living with my best friend back in Baltimore, until I get a permanent place here in January Cove."

"Name?"

She sighed and then laughed. "Rigoletto."

"Riggo...what?"

"Rigoletto. It's an opera by Verde. Based on a play by Victor Hugo..." she said, as if she was trying to jog his memory. "You've never heard of it?"

"Um, no. We don't get into stuff like that 'round these parts, ma'am," he said in a fake, thick Southern accent that sounded nothing like his own easy way of talking.

"Very funny."

"What's it about?"

"Do you really want to know or are you being sarcastic?"

"I really want to know. It would do me good to learn something new."

"Well, it's an opera in three acts. I think it first opened in eighteen fifty-one. It's a tragic tale with secrets and seduction and a curse and even assassins."

"Wow. Maybe I need to see that one."

"Really?" she asked, turning her head just long enough to see him watching her intently.

"I might need a beer first. And a translation guide. And some caffeine. And toothpicks to hold up my eyelids. But yeah, I'd let you take me to that."

Her breath caught in her throat. "Take you? To an opera? Just me and you?"

"Well, I don't think anyone else would want to go. And I don't think they would allow your dog to come, right?"

She laughed. "Don't worry. I don't know anywhere that even puts on Rigoletto around here. I think you're safe."

"Turn here," he said as they made their way down the road. She pulled into the parking lot and found a space as close to the front door as she could. "Well, for what it's worth, I would go just to see your eyes light up watching it. This is the first time I've seen you really get excited about something."

Her heart clenched. "You haven't really known me very long."

He leaned in and spoke softly. "I've known you long enough to know that you deserve to being doing more than just living someone else's dreams, Laura."

She froze in place, her face just inches from his. "Um…"

"Are you ready?" he asked softly, his breath literally lapping at her lips.

"Ready? For what?" she asked, her breath ragged and strained.

"For my therapy appointment?" he responded

with a smile as he leaned back. Oh, this guy knew just what he was doing. Laura pursed her lips.

"Of course," she said several octaves higher than her normal voice. "Why wouldn't I be? Let me come around and open your door."

After helping him out of the car - without touching him any more than she had to - she pulled his crutches from the back seat and helped him get steady.

"I'll be out here when you're finished," she said, shutting the passenger door.

"I thought you might come inside with me?" he asked, smiling and shrugging his shoulders.

"Sawyer, you don't need me in there."

"Moral support?"

She stood there with her hands on her hips before finally relenting to his request. "Fine. But don't embarrass me."

GOING to physical therapy with Sawyer had turned out to be very eye-opening. His pain was a lot worse than she had imagined. The therapist had worked with him for almost an hour, pulling his arm in different directions and stretching out the muscle.

He had also talked about doing something called dry needling, which didn't sound at all pleasant in Laura's mind. She felt very sorry for him, especially knowing that she had caused the pain he was currently in.

The good news was that he would be out of the sling in just a few days. They were also able to prescribe something for the pain and to help loosen up his muscles. Thankfully, it wasn't anything addictive and he would only have to take it for a week or two.

"Thanks again for bringing me to my therapy appointment. I know you'll be busy opening your store in another few days, so I'll catch a ride from somebody for my other appointments."

Laura helped him into the car, sliding his crutches into the back seat and shutting the door. "No, I don't mind at all. I'm sure that I can give you a ride the next time too."

She walked around and slipped behind the driver's seat, shutting her door. Before she cranked the car, she glanced over at Sawyer who was looking at her and smiling.

"What?"

"Did you think we would end up actually being friends after the way that we met?"

Laura laughed. "Is that what we are? We're friends?"

He furrowed his eyebrows and cocked his head to the side. "You don't think we're friends?"

"I guess so. I just don't know you very well yet."

"Well, let's remedy that. How about some lunch?"

"Lunch?"

"Yes, it's the meal after breakfast and before supper."

"Ha ha. You're a regular comedian. I guess we could go grab some lunch."

"See? Lunch is something that friends do." Sawyer laughed as they drove down the road in search of a great place to eat.

A FEW MINUTES later they pulled into one of the most popular restaurants in town, Zach's. Sawyer seemed really happy to be able to eat there. According to him, they had the best chili cheese fries he'd ever had in his life.

Laura was excited to learn a little bit more about him. He seemed kind of mysterious, like he was hiding something from his past or maybe even his present. Of course, she had no idea what that could be.

Seemed like everybody in town knew him but he had grown up there so that was nothing unusual. And everyone seemed to like him, so she didn't think he had some kind of sordid past. Maybe she would get around to asking somebody about him, but that seemed almost a little bit stalker-ish and she didn't want to come off as even being interested in him.

"I'm so happy to be able to eat here again. It's

been many years since I've gotten to come to Zach's."
Sawyer took a long sip of his sweet tea. "We used to
eat here after every football game in high school. See
those pictures on the wall? I bet you'll find a few of
me and Brad, and maybe Jackson too."

"Everything on the menu looks really good," she
said as she stared at all of the choices.

"So, tell me more about yourself, Laura. What
was your life like back in Baltimore?"

She thought for a moment about what to say.
Should she tell the truth? Should she make it sound
better than it really was? But she decided that if they
really were going to be friends – and she definitely
needed more friends in January Cove – that she
should probably be as honest as possible.

"Well, I was married for a long time and now I'm
divorced. I worked at a marketing company, but it
turned out to be just about the most boring job in
the world. My best friend and I have known each
other since we were in elementary school. And you
know about my mother and my dog. So... that's
about it."

Sawyer smiled. "I have a feeling there's a lot more
to you than meets the eye."

"I have the same feeling about you," she said, a
hint of sarcasm in her voice.

"Oh really? I assure you there is not a whole lot
more here than meets the eye." He smiled that
lopsided grin, and she wondered for a moment if

he'd notice her putting the side of her cold drinking glass across her forehead.

The server interrupted them to get their food order. Of course, Sawyer took that chance to order chili cheese fries. Laura got a club sandwich, but fully planned to sample his food when it arrived.

"Okay then. Tell me more about yourself. Before you came back to January Cove, where were you living?" she asked.

He seemed to fidget around in his seat, a sure sign that he was uncomfortable. She already knew that much about him. "Well, I was a struggling musician in Nashville."

"Nashville? I've never been there but I've heard great things about it. Struggling? What does that mean exactly?"

"Well, let's just say that the people out there didn't want to make the same kind of music I do."

"Country, you mean?"

"Not exactly. I like country, but I just wanted to be a little more progressive. Maybe a little too controversial for that scene."

She could tell he was being evasive and that he was highly uncomfortable with the conversation, but she didn't know why. It just didn't make any sense to her that this guy, who was really friendly with her, didn't want to tell her anything about his recent past.

"So, where does that leave you now? Did you just come back here to visit your friends?"

"Sort of. You know, sometimes you just need to go home to recharge your batteries. I'm not sure what the future holds, but I know that music will be involved."

"Well, I can't wait to hear you play and sing. I bet you're really good."

He took another sip of his tea. "I hope I don't disappoint you."

"So you know it will involve music, but are you saying you might not go back to Nashville?"

"Possibly. I just haven't made that decision yet. Sometimes, life feels like there's a fork in the road and you have to make a decision. I'm just not sure what decision I'll make yet. Know what I mean?"

"Um, remember I'm here to chase my dead mother's dreams, so I understand making a tough decision at a fork in the road." Sawyer laughed at that.

They continued chatting about random things, mostly gossip around town. Sawyer filled her in on all of the major players in the Parker family as well as some other people throughout the town that she needed to know. He encouraged her to make friends with Rebecca, who owned the coffee shop called Jolt. Rebecca was dating Jackson Parker, the eldest child of the Parker family and the one who had taken care of his siblings after their father died when they were young.

They talked about the area, its history and a lot of other surface things that, although important for her to know, didn't really get to the root of who Sawyer was. But she decided not to pull on that string any more than she had to. The guy was obviously uncomfortable and she wasn't going to push it. She knew how that felt – being pushed when you aren't ready to do something or talk about something.

"So, Laura, I've been thinking about something. I want to make you an offer."

"An offer? Why do I not like the sound of this?" she laughed.

"I think you'll like this offer. I appreciate you taking me to physical therapy, so I want to return the favor."

"Favor? I hit you with my car. I think that I owed you at least that. I think we should also stop keeping score because this is getting confusing."

He smiled that crooked smile, one dimple appearing on the corner of his mouth and making her stomach flip-flop. Since it was full of chili fries that she had stolen from his plate, that wasn't a good thing.

"Here's what I'm offering. Since I have nothing else to do, I would like to help you at your bakery when it opens."

She was impressed by his kind gesture, but had to wonder how a one armed, one legged man was going to help her open what would hopefully be a very busy bakery.

"Do you think that you're in any position to do that?" she asked in the nicest way she knew how.

"Are you saying that I'm unable to work? I've got one arm and I'm sure you have a stool. Let me at least help by bringing people food or putting stuff in bags. I'm going crazy sitting in my house all the time. I'm not used to all of this down time. It would really be doing me a service."

She sat for a moment and thought about his offer. She really could use the help since she had no money to hire anyone right now. She wanted to keep as much of the money that she'd left Baltimore with, and the money from the house hadn't come through fully yet. So, having a little bit of free help would be a godsend right now, even if he might not be back to 100%.

"All right then. I will gladly accept the help."

"Great! So what time would you like me to arrive for work tomorrow, boss?"

"How about 8 AM?"

"Sounds good to me. Of course, that means you have to pick me up at 7:45 tomorrow, right?" he said with a laugh.

"Are you going to make this a habit? Of me being your taxi service?"

"Maybe so."

CHAPTER 7

After they finished eating, Laura insisted on paying the check. After all, she knew that running into him with her car had probably caused him some medical bills that exceeded his insurance. He argued at first, insisting that the man was supposed to pay, but she finally convinced the chivalrous Southern man that they weren't on a date so that rule didn't apply.

"I'm sorry, ma'am, I'm going to need to see your driver's license also." The server stood by the table, blonde hair pulled back in a perfect ponytail. She watched to see if Sawyer would look at the woman, who was obviously gorgeous and made straight from the hands of God, but he didn't even flinch. Instead, she noticed him looking at her driver's license as she laid it on the table.

The waitress walked away with the license and

the credit card. "I wrote on the back that they should check my license, just so no one could forge my signature. Had someone fraudulently use my card a couple of years ago."

"You're a very careful type of person aren't you, Laura?" he asked with a quirk of a smile.

"I guess so. It's served me well over the years though," she insisted.

"Has it? Really?"

"Don't start an argument, Sawyer. We had such a nice lunch together."

"I'm not trying to start an argument. I'm just asking if being so safe all the time has really served you well? I mean, have you done all the things in your life that you want to do?"

"What kind of a question is that? Of course I haven't. No one has."

"True. We should all have goals for every stage of life, but do you really think that being safe all the time is going to allow you to achieve your dreams?"

"I don't know. My ex-husband used to say something similar. So does my best friend. I guess I just like knowing that whatever I'm about to do it's going to be the right thing, so sometimes I get paralyzed by thinking about it all and I don't make *any* moves."

"I noticed something on your driver's license."

"That is my real weight! I did not lie on my driver's license. I probably put on a couple of pounds since I came to town..."

"Relax, Laura! I wasn't talking about your weight. I was talking about your birthday. Do you realize that you're six months older than me?"

"I am? But, I thought…"

"That I was older than you?"

"Kind of…" she smiled sheepishly.

"It's okay. I choose to believe that all the smiling I do causes these little lines around my eyes, so I don't mind them much." He pointed to the beginnings of crow's feet on his face.

She stared for a moment at the crow's feet that were just starting to form on the edges of his eyes. They were handsome and sexy and rugged and everything about them was great. And she definitely needed to go take a cold shower.

SAWYER STOOD at the kitchen counter of the small beach cottage he was renting, leaning against the granite countertops and trying to steady himself. "Look, I realize they don't like that I've walked away from my whole life there, but I'm not going to make music that I don't like. I'm just not that kind of person. I'm sure they can find someone on one of those reality TV talent shows who will replace me in a heartbeat, but I just don't have any interest in coming back anytime soon."

"Man, if you don't come back soon, you are going

to lose everything you worked so hard for. I don't get it. What's wrong with you? You can't just walk away from all of this. You have fans..."

"I appreciate my real fans, but the ones who are flaky and fair weather and didn't like my latest album? I don't think those are really my fans. I don't think I really fit into that scene. Fame just isn't for me."

Even as he said it, he was surprised to hear it come out of his mouth. He'd never said that before. He had enjoyed being famous at the beginning, but it got old really fast.

Not being able to walk around outside without someone taking his picture or asking for selfie. Not being able to take a woman out to a restaurant and have a decent meal because he was constantly being bombarded with people asking for autographs.

The money had been good, and he enjoyed his true fans for a time. But Sawyer was realizing that he wanted to go back to his regular life. His simple life. His life in January Cove.

The only problem was he didn't know where he fit into the world anymore. He loved music. Singing. Playing his guitar. Those were all things he couldn't live without. They were like breathing to him. But he didn't know how to incorporate those into January Cove. It wasn't exactly a hotbed of the music world.

What was he supposed to do now? Play at the

local coffee shop on Friday nights? He needed something to do, something that would bring in an income and allow him to still express his love of music.

Nashville had been a wonderful place, a place he would always call his second home. But making music to someone else's standards just didn't work for him. He had been a highly trained musician, and he wanted to be able to use those skills and talents in a way that felt natural and authentic to him.

Dylan had been his best friend in Nashville, and he had tried repeatedly now to talk Sawyer into coming back. Giving it another chance. Maybe finding a different agent or recording label. But Sawyer wasn't swayed. The longer he remained in January Cove, the more he felt attached to it again.

It was funny, really. All of the years of growing up in January Cove had made him want to leave. To pursue bigger dreams in bigger places with bigger people. But in the end, all he really wanted to do was come back home and live a simpler life, playing his guitar and singing to people who cared.

The thing was, he had plenty of money to basically retire and stay in January Cove if he wanted to, but twiddling his thumbs wasn't what he wanted to do either.

And if he was honest with himself, he wanted to get to know Laura Bennett more. He wanted to find out about her, and all the emotional traumas she'd been through in her life. Find out what was at the core of her being. Touch her with his music. See her succeed in her bakery.

And he didn't know why he cared so damn much about someone he just met.

What he did know was that he'd never felt this way about a woman so soon. He'd never felt like he needed to stay close and spend more time with a woman he just met, especially one who had almost killed him with her car.

Even though he was in pain, every time he thought about the fact that they'd met that way, it made him smile. He could see thirty years into the future, telling their grandchildren the story.

"Dude? Are you even listening to me?"

Dylan shattered his happy thoughts of sitting on a porch swing with Laura decades in the future while the grandchildren ran through the front yard hunting Easter eggs or picking berries from their fruit trees.

"Yes, I'm listening to you. I always listen to you. And we'll be buddies for the rest of our lives, Dylan. But, I don't think I'm coming back to Nashville."

"You know I love you, man, but I think you're making the biggest mistake of your life. You're letting go of something that you worked so hard to build, and I just think you're going to come to regret it."

Sawyer thought for a moment, but he definitely

believed that Dylan was wrong about that. In fact, coming home to January Cove had been the only decision in his entire life that he was one-hundred percent sure was right.

"I'll talk to you later, okay?"

Sawyer ended the call and thought about the situation with Laura. She had no idea who he was. She wasn't a fan of country music, and so far he'd been able to keep his identity under wraps.

He was never really sure why he was doing it. At first, he didn't want some crazed fan following him around town but then when he realized that she didn't like country music and didn't know who he was, it felt nice. It felt good to have someone like him for just who he was. Not because of his fame. Not because of his money. Not even because he was one of the most popular guys in January Cove. Just because he was Sawyer.

At least he thought that she liked him. He had no idea what this woman was feeling. There'd been a moment in the car, a moment where he struggled not to just lean over and kiss her full on the mouth. He wasn't sure if she felt the same or was just uncomfortable that this creepy guy she barely knew was leaning in so close to her.

She was a hard one to figure out, a puzzle he wanted to solve.

He knew what he had to do, and it would take some maneuvering around town. But he had to make sure that everyone who knew Laura and knew him would keep his secret for the short term. He'd eventually tell her, and hope that she wasn't mad at him for keeping such a secret. But for now he just wanted to be Sawyer, not Sawyer the mega country music superstar.

He just wanted to be a man who was attracted to a woman and wanted to see where it would go without any complications.

Surely, that had to work.

~

"So LET me get this straight. You want me to not tell Laura Bennett that you're a famous country music singer?" Addison said as Sawyer sat on the other side of the table with a pleading look on his face. Clay leaned back in his chair with his arms crossed.

"Man, you know this is never going to work. This is going to blow up in your face," Clay said. "Secrets always have a way of doing that." He looked over at Addison who nodded knowingly. Sawyer didn't know exactly what that was about.

"I know it won't work long-term. I'm just asking you to temporarily not tell her. Of course, if she asks you, then I don't expect you to lie. Just don't offer up the information, okay?" Thankfully, Laura was across the street at the bakery getting things set up for opening day.

"Fine. I'll do what you ask, but not for long. She deserves to know, especially if you to end up getting involved," Addison said.

"Getting involved? I highly doubt that. I don't even think she's interested in me."

"Are you kidding me? Of course she is. It's written all over her face every time you're around each other. It makes me want to spray air freshener when you to leave because it's so thick in the room."

Little Anna Grace came running into the room at that point, screeching about something and giggling. Clay and Addison were immediately distracted by the cuteness of their daughter. And it gave Sawyer a reason to leave.

"If you'd do me a favor and let the rest of the Parkers know, especially your brother Brad, I'd appreciate it. Kind of hard to get around town on these things," he said, holding one crutch in the air.

"Brad? I can't promise anything with him," Addison said laughing.

"Just do the best you can. I owe you one," Sawyer said, leaning down and giving her a quick kiss on the top of her head before maneuvering his way back outside on his crutches.

As soon as he hit the door, he saw Laura walking across the street, looking exhausted.

"Wow. You look like you could use a break," he said. It was almost dinnertime, and Laura's business was opening the next morning. Sawyer had been helping her for the last couple of days, mainly just getting things set up in the bakery. He wasn't much help, although he was finally able to stop wearing his sling for a few hours at a time now that the medication was helping to loosen his muscles.

But still, being on crutches really hampered him from doing a whole lot, including lifting heavy stuff around the bakery.

"I am very tired," she said, slumping down onto the top step in front of the inn.

"Can I interest you in some dinner?" he asked with a hopeful smile.

"Dinner? I don't know about that. I really don't feel like getting all freshened up to go out to a restaurant tonight, but thanks for the offer."

"No, I mean if I cooked dinner for you?"

Laura looked surprised. "You cook?"

"Well, I try. I make a mean hamburger and home-made french fries. How do you feel about that?"

"That sounds heavenly right now. Let me at least go brush through my hair and we can leave."

As she walked in the house, Sawyer sat outside and wondered what in the world he was getting himself into. Maybe Dylan was right. He'd just given up a lucrative career doing the very thing he loved to come home to a small town and find a woman that was making him quiver on the inside.

But for once, he was leaping out into the

unknown without a plan whatsoever. And he had no idea how this whole thing was going to end.

WHEN THEY ARRIVED at Sawyer's house, Laura was uneasy. *What is she getting herself into?* She was already busy trying to open her bakery and figure out ways that she could live out her mother's dreams, so what in the world was she doing having dinner with this man that she was extremely attracted to?

It just seemed like a bad idea. After all, he was probably only in town for a short time trying to figure himself out. Trying to figure out what he wanted to do next. Licking his wounds from being a failed music artist.

She just didn't know if she had time for this, but she so wanted to be in the presence of a man who was interested in her. Someone who asked her questions and really cared about the answers. Someone with the jaw line that looked like it could cut glass and steely blue eyes that made her want to melt.

"The burgers should be done in a few minutes," Sawyer said as he flopped down into the armchair next to where she was sitting on the sofa.

"How's your arm?" she asked, pointing to his injured arm that no longer had the sling.

"Good. I've been doing the exercises that the

therapist showed me and taking my muscle relaxant, so it seems to be helping a lot. When you open tomorrow, I might actually be able to use two hands. That's progress!"

"Well, I also know what that means."

"What does it mean?" he asked, raising an eyebrow.

"It means that you can play your guitar for me after dinner, right? You promised."

"He smiled.

"I'd be delighted to. It's been a long time since I've been able to play."

"How long?"

"Since you hit me with your car," he said with a laugh.

DINNER CONVERSATION HAD BEEN light and easygoing, much like lunch. Sawyer had asked her a lot of questions about her job and why she found it so boring. She asked him about growing up in January Cove all those years ago.

"Those burgers were amazing," Laura said, leaning back in her chair and toying with the idea of unbuttoning the top of her capri pants. She thought better of it, not wanting to forget and lose her pants when she stood up next.

"Thank you. It's the one thing my father taught

me that I still use in my life," he said with an ironic laugh.

"You didn't have a good relationship with your father?" Laura took a sip of the sweet tea he'd made, and it was more like syrup than the tea she was used to up North. Still, it was growing on her already.

"No, not really. When I was a little kid, it was okay, but he was never really interested in being a Dad, ya know? He was more interested in women. Lots and lots of women. Mainly younger ones. My mother died when I was in preschool, so I don't really remember her, but I remember my father just bringing woman after woman home."

"I'm sorry. Is he still alive?"

"I guess so. Honestly, I don't know. He got married three times before I made it to high school. Then he decided to follow a woman out to Arizona and left me here with my great aunt. Thank God, because she was an amazing woman, and it allowed me to stay here in January Cove."

"When's the last time you heard from him?"

His jaw clenched a bit, and Laura could tell she'd struck a nerve. "Years ago."

She decided to let it go. "So, cowboy, are you ready to play for me?"

"Cowboy?"

"I don't know. Sounded good in my head," she said, closing her eyes. "I'm so tired."

"I bet you are. Listen, we can do this another

night. You don't have to sit here and listen to me play. You need to get back to Addy's and get some sleep."

Laura looked down at her watch. It was only seven-thirty, and she knew if she went back now, she'd just end up watching Netflix for a few hours instead of sleeping. She was far too excited and anxious about her opening the next morning.

"No, I really want to hear you. If you don't mind, that is?"

"Of course I don't mind. Music notes run through these veins," he said, holding out his forearm. She noticed the thick veins, so masculine and strong. Ted never had veins like that. Even his veins were wimpy, she thought.

Sawyer stood and walked to the corner, picking up his guitar, before returning to the arm chair next to the sofa. The sun was starting to make its descent outside, with wisps of yellow and orange peeking through the partially opened mini blinds.

Without a word, he started playing the guitar. It took him a moment to situate himself so that he didn't strain his vulnerable arm, but once he got going, he was amazing. Laura stared at him in awe, amazed at his technique. She knew next to nothing about playing the guitar, but he seemed to be an expert at it.

He didn't look at her, instead staring down at his hands and then closing his eyes as if he and the instrument were involved in some intimate dance and she was an intruder.

And then he began to sing.

Dear God, his voice. It was soulful and soothing at the same time. Perfect pitch and tone. A gravely quality that drew her in and made her want to listen to him forever and a day. It was like a warm bath that flowed through her entire body. How could he possibly have failed in Nashville? He was everything that a musician should be.

The song he sang was country in sound to some extent, but there was a bluesy component that reached deep down into her soul and tugged at the strings of her own heart. She could feel his words, but she also felt the music in a way that even classical had never touched.

When he finished playing the song, Laura realized that she had tears running down her cheeks. She tried to quickly wipe them away so she wouldn't look like an idiot, but it was too late. Sawyer stopped, obviously worried that he'd upset her somehow and put the guitar aside as he slid to the end of his chair.

"Are you okay?" he asked softly. "I didn't mean to upset you."

Laura smiled, wiping the last tear from her now reddening cheeks. "I'm fine. I just wasn't expecting... that."

"Expecting what?"

"Something so... beautiful. I can't even describe what that did to me. Sawyer, you are so amazingly talented. I can't even..."

She stumbled over her words, getting more embarrassed by the second.

"Thank you," he said, his voice sounding like it was about to break. "That means a lot."

He cleared his throat and she did the same, both of them trying to move past the moments of awkward silence where neither knew what to say.

"I could literally listen to that all night. Maybe you could make me a recording?"

He laughed. It was an ironic laugh, and she didn't understand it, but it definitely wasn't a typical laugh. She decided not to dig further for the moment.

"How about you lie back right there on the sofa, and I'll play until you tell me to stop?"

That sounded heavenly to her at the moment, so she took the invitation to recline back on the sofa and listen to the sweet, sexy sounds of Sawyer serenading her. And in that moment, she silently thanked her best friend for urging her to go to January Cove.

CHAPTER 8

It was dark, with just flickers of light occasionally darting around the room. The sound of breathing was the only noise. His arm ached, and his leg was going numb.

Sawyer forced open his eyes, wondering what kind of weird dream he was having. But it wasn't a dream.

He was crammed into the arm chair, his guitar lying on the floor next to him. His guitar. He'd been playing and singing. And Laura... she'd been lying on his sofa. And she still was.

She looked so peaceful in the silhouette of moonlight, a small smile still painted on her face. She was snuggled into a patchwork blanket his great aunt had sewn with her aging hands, and that made his heart smile.

On her side, she was facing his direction, the

blanket pulled up under her neck. He checked the clock. It was almost midnight, and she needed to get home and get some sleep in a regular bed. His sofa wasn't exactly the most comfortable place on Earth.

Still, he just wanted to look at her. She was beautiful with her long, dirty blond hair and perfect skin. And when her eyes were open, they were a stunning version of emerald green mixed with flecks of gold.

This had been one of the best nights of his life, which was ironic and amusing at the same time. He had played some of the biggest venues in the country, yet this night playing for one pretty woman in his tiny rented living room was one of his favorite nights ever.

He'd sung a song for her that the critics had panned, and fans hadn't understood. It was a darker song, more bluesy, more real than anything he'd sang before. And Laura had cried. Real tears had flowed from her amazing eyes. She had understood him and who he was from just one song.

It meant more to him than all the screaming fans and royalty checks he'd accumulated over the last few years. Her smile. Her tears. Their connection.

And it had taken everything in him not to kiss her on the spot. But the last thing he wanted to do was assume she felt the same about him or to scare her away. Just because his music touched her didn't mean she wanted *him* to touch her.

He leaned closer, not wanting to scare her but

realizing she needed to get back to the inn. "Laura?" he whispered, but she only stirred. She was so tired, and he hated to wake her up. "Laura?" he repeated, brushing a strand of hair that had fallen onto her eyes.

She roused a bit and squinted at him as if she was confused before jolting straight up and looking around.

"It's okay. You're at my house, remember?" Sawyer said, sliding next to her on the sofa. He turned on the small table lamp beside the couch.

"Oh. I'm so sorry I fell asleep listening to you," she said with a tired smile as she rubbed her eyes and then yawned. "I guess I was more tired than I thought."

"You can sleep on my sofa anytime," he said without thinking. "I mean...Actually, I don't know what that meant."

Laura laughed. "I'd better get back. I'm surprised Addison hasn't sent a search party out looking for me yet. Where's my phone?" She rummaged around on the sofa until she found it at the bottom of the blanket. The screen lit up when she touched it, revealing unread text messages.

"Everything okay?" Sawyer asked when he saw the look of alarm on her face.

"Oh no... Oh no..."

"Laura, what's wrong?"

"Addy texted me hours ago and said there was a

power outage on that whole side of the street. She was worried my refrigerator would be off and ruin the cupcakes for tomorrow. I've got to get to the store!"

She jumped up and started looking for her shoes which she had tossed across the living room at some point before falling asleep.

"I'm going with you," Sawyer said, standing up and reaching for his crutches.

"No. No. It's fine. You need to rest up for tomorrow, and I…"

Sawyer reached for her arm and turned her around. "Laura, I'm going. I don't want you in the store alone at night."

"It's January Cove," she said. "No one is going to bother me."

"I'm going."

"Fine. I don't have time to argue with you," she said, searching for her purse.

The irony was that he couldn't fight off an attacker if he wanted to, and she probably thought the same thing, but he wasn't ready to let Laura go for the night anyway. If it meant sitting in the darkened bakery, icing cupcakes until dawn, that was exactly what he'd do.

LAURA AND SAWYER raced over to the bakery in the dead of night. By the time they got there, it was almost 12:30 and the street was dark. Apparently, the power had been out for quite a few hours for some unknown reason. Of course, it had to be the night before she was opening her very first business.

She felt defeated, but she also knew that she couldn't give up. Having Sawyer there took some of the pressure off, at least.

"I don't know what I'm going to do," she said as she sorted through the refrigerator. Most of the cupcakes weren't completely ruined, but they certainly weren't of the quality that she wanted to display to her customers on opening day.

"You don't think you can salvage any of these?" Sawyer asked as he helped her sort through the multicolored and multi-flavored cupcakes using the light of their cell phones.

Laura hung her head in her hands. She was so tired and yet so wired about her opening. As if God was sending her a sign, the power popped back on.

"I don't see how I can make this work. I spent hours and hours making these yesterday morning. There's no way I'm going to have time to get enough made to replace these. Maybe I should just delay my opening..."

"No. I'll help you. Just show me what to do."

"I can't ask you to do that," she said, standing up and leaning against the counter. "I know you're tired too, and you need some sleep before we open up tomorrow as well."

Sawyer stood and faced her, bags starting to form under his eyes. "Listen, I'll do whatever you need me to do to make sure that this is a success. I can sleep later," he said, putting his hand on her arm. God, it felt good to have a man touch her, even if it was just her arm.

The gesture meant more to her than he would probably ever know. Ted had never gone out of his way to help her follow her dreams. If he were there right now, she knew there'd be no way he would stand in the gap with her and make sure that her bakery had a successful opening. He would go home, probably watch some sporting event and then go to bed, leaving her in the lurch to handle things. After all, cooking and baking would be considered woman's work in Ted's eyes.

"Okay then. I guess we should get started," Laura relented.

Sawyer smiled. "All right, fearless leader, tell me what I need to do!" His forced enthusiasm in the wee hours of the morning was almost contagious. Almost.

"Well, thankfully I mixed up a huge batch of the flour I need to create the batter. So we can mix that with the liquids and get several pans into the ovens right now…"

She began showing him exactly what to do,

although stirring was a bit of an issue. In that moment, she thanked God for industrial sized mixers.

"The next step, while those are cooking, is that we need to mix up the icing for the different types of cupcakes we're making. I was going to open with five different kinds to match the batter. My mother taught me most of these recipes, so I'm swearing you to secrecy," she said with a smile.

"I'm a little scared of you anyway, so I promise that I won't reveal your secrets." Sawyer winked at her, and her legs went weak. She convinced herself it was just the overwhelming fatigue she was feeling.

They spent the next two hours baking and mixing and icing dozens of cupcakes. By the time they were finished, it was almost four in the morning and Laura was about to fall on her face with exhaustion.

"I guess that's it. We've done all we can do," she said, staring down at the cupcakes laid out before them. Since the power had come back on shortly after they had arrived at the bakery, the refrigerator was cold enough to finally put the cupcakes back into it.

"If I never see another cupcake again, it might be too soon," Sawyer said with a wry smile.

"Don't say that!" Laura said, jabbing his midsection with one of her fingers. Gosh, how could anything be that rock solid?

"So, I'm going to head back to Addy's and get at least a little bit of sleep. I hope I don't wake them up when I go into the house…"

"I'm sure with a small child they are probably up and down throughout the night. But you are welcome to come stay at my place if you want. I'll sleep on the sofa…" Sawyer offered.

"No thanks. I appreciate the offer, but I don't want to look like this when I meet my customers in a few hours," Laura said, pointing to her flour covered shirt.

Sawyer smiled. "I don't know, I think it's kind of a cute look."

Her insides were starting to turn to mush, and the sugar rush was getting to her head so she decided that she better make her way across the street before she did something she might come to regret.

"Well then, have a good sleep," Sawyer said. "And, Laura?"

"Yes?"

"I had fun with you these last few hours," he said, winking at her before he walked toward the front door.

As she locked up and made her way across the street to the bed-and-breakfast, Sawyer stood on the corner of the street, watching her safely inside.

THE NEXT MORNING WAS A BLUR. Laura had been running on fumes and adrenaline and probably a little bit too much cupcake icing, but the opening had been a success.

She and Sawyer barely had a chance to talk because he was ringing up customers and she was wrapping up cupcakes, but at the end of the day when they locked the door, it had been an amazing success.

"People loved your cupcakes!" Sawyer said smiling as Laura turned around after locking the door for the day.

"I think they did," she said incredulously, a huge grin painted on her still exhausted face. "I really can't believe that went so well considering what happened last night, but I think this might actually be a success. I just can't believe it..."

"You can't believe it? Why?" Sawyer asked as he sat down on one of the retro looking barstools against the wall.

"I don't know. I've always worked for somebody else. I was never the one calling the shots, and honestly I didn't think I could do this. At least my ex-husband didn't think I could do this." Laura sat down next to him.

"Well, he's an idiot then."

Laura laughed. "I like the way you put that."

"I don't know about you, but I'm feeling pretty gross right now, so I think I'm going to head home and take a hot shower."

Images of Sawyer taking a shower floated through her mind, and Laura physically shook her head to get rid of them.

"Yes, I think I'm going to go to the same. Listen, thank you so much for helping me last night and all day today. I really appreciate it. I feel hopeful about this," she said, waving her hand around at the store.

"See you tomorrow?" Sawyer said as he stood up. He was doing much better on his crutches and would probably only be on them another week or two according to the physical therapist.

"Do you want me to drive you home?" she offered. In reality, as much as she liked hanging out with him, she really just wanted to sink into a hot bath and then take a nice long nap.

"No. I think I'll take a walk."

After he left, Laura finished cleaning up and then started to make her way across the street. Her cell phone rang, and she looked down to see that it was Carrie.

"Hello?"

"So how did it go?" Carrie asked. Of course her best friend wouldn't forget that she was opening her business that morning.

"It went fantastic! We had a great turnout, and people had lots of nice things to say about the cupcakes."

"And which one was their favorite?"

"Of course it was the birthday cake batter!" Laura said, proving her friend right when they'd made a bet the day before on which one would be the most popular.

"See? I'm the smartest person you know!" Carrie said laughing. "So, how's it going with loverboy?"

"Would you quit saying that?"

"Why? It's true!"

Laura sighed. "He's a nice guy. We're friends. That is all."

"Sure. Okay."

"So when are you coming to visit me?"

"I'm not sure. I've taken on a few new coaching clients so I've been really busy every day, but it's not like I can't do my business on the road."

"Well, be sure to let me know before you come because I can't wait to see you, and I'll be sure to make extra birthday cake batter cupcakes before you get here!"

Truthfully, she really did miss her best friend. They'd spent almost every day together since they were in elementary school, so it'd been quite an adjustment to not have her there to rely on. Having Sawyer as a friend did help to fill that gap a little bit, but it wasn't the same as sitting at a lunch table every day talking to her best girlfriend about all of life's trials and tribulations.

Laura hung up the phone with her friend and walked into the bed-and-breakfast and straight up the stairs. As much as she loved Addison and Clay, she didn't want to interact with anyone. She really just wanted to sink down into her hot bath and relax after a long hard day.

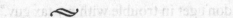

THE NEXT WEEK WAS A BLUR, with Sawyer and Laura working side-by-side at the cupcake shop. He had to admit that it was a lot of fun talking to people from town while trying to stay out of the limelight.

There had been a couple of close calls with people almost saying his full name or asking for an autograph or picture, but thankfully most of the people who lived in January Cove just saw him as Sawyer - the irritating kid that went to high school there and chased girls. Most people there didn't see him as some kind of big superstar, and he hoped to keep it that way.

Working with Laura had also made him even more sure that he was interested in her in a way that was more than friendship, but he couldn't really tell if she felt the same. She was all business when they were at work, although she was friendly to everyone who came in.

"What's your last name?" she asked out of the blue.

"What?"

"It just dawned on me that I don't know your last

name and you're working here. I probably should fill out some paperwork for you," she said with a smile.

"How do you know I don't go by just one name? Like Madonna or Cher?" he said wryly.

"Seriously. I need to put it on paperwork so I don't get in trouble with my tax guy."

"You're not paying me."

She cocked her head to the side, a confused look on her face. "Is there something wrong? Is there some reason you don't want me to know your last name?"

It dawned on Sawyer that if he kept pushing the issue, she'd probably just go to Google and look up his name thinking he was some kind of ax murderer or escaped convict.

"Griffin. My last name is Griffin."

"Sawyer Griffin. Gosh, that sounds so familiar to me."

His hands were starting to sweat. Why was he hiding this from her? They knew each other well enough now that she probably wouldn't think anything of his celebrity status, but yet he still felt like he wanted to keep it from her for a little while longer. He wanted to forge a relationship without her knowing who he was. Without her having any preconceived notions about him. He liked that when she looked at him, she saw *him* and not some caricature of a celebrity.

"Sounds familiar? I can't imagine why."

"Oh! I know!"

Sawyer's stomach clenched. She knew? He braced himself.

"I knew a guy back in Baltimore whose name was Griffin Sawyer. He delivered our mail at the office. Isn't that weird? What a small world!" she said before she went back to wiping down the counters. He let out the breath that he had been unknowingly holding.

The next customer walked in. It was a woman, a little bit older than they were, who looked stressed out about something. She was distracted, to say the least.

"Welcome to Sweetcakes!" Laura said, as she did to every customer. The woman smiled, her eyes darting around to what was in the refrigerated case, before she finally looked at Laura.

"I'll take one of the red velvet," she said.

"Is everything okay?" she asked the woman.

The woman smiled sadly. "Yes. No, actually. It's been a very rough day, to be honest."

"I'm sorry. Is there anything I can do to help you?" Laura had been really trying to make connections with people in the community, and Sawyer had been impressed by her level of empathy when people were having a bad day.

"Not unless you know someone who's looking for a job as a music teacher," she said with a sigh. Laura immediately cut her eyes to Sawyer.

125

"Music?" Sawyer said, unable to keep himself from getting involved.

"Yes. Do you know someone?"

"I might. What exactly does it involve?" he asked, pulling his Sweetcakes baseball cap down further over his eyes.

"Well, I own a nonprofit organization. We teach kids how to play different instruments, especially kids who are from underprivileged areas. We had someone all set up to run the program here in January Cove, but her father became ill and she ended up having to move across the country to take care of him. Now we're kind of left in the lurch because we have a summer camp starting in July with twenty-five kids signed up and no one to run it."

Sawyer was nervous. This woman didn't seem to recognize him, but it was only a matter of time if he took over the program before people started noticing who he was. It would be almost impossible to keep his secret from Laura, so if he took the position he might have to tell her sooner than he thought.

"Well, I'm very well-versed in the guitar. And I sing. I've got some training from college myself..."

"He's being modest. Sawyer is an amazing musician, and your kids would be so lucky to have him as their teacher," Laura said.

The woman's eyes lit up. "Then it seems like it

would be fantastic! You sound perfect. Look, I'm in a hurry for doctor's appointment, but let me give you my card. If you can give me a call, maybe later today?"

Sawyer looked at Laura, who was grinning from ear to ear. He took the woman's card and assured her that he would be calling. But inside, he didn't know what he was going to do.

CHAPTER 9

Sawyer called the woman about the music
position that evening. They agreed to meet
up in a few days, which would give him time to tell
Laura who he really was. But he didn't want to.

She treated him like a "normal" person. Not a
celebrity, and not the former kid from January Cove.
It was a unique feeling to spend time with a woman
who wasn't after him for his fame. Or former fame,
so it was.

Everyday, he struggled with the decision he'd
made to walk away from a lucrative career that he
had dreamed about for so many years. The money
had been good.

Yet, there were still times that he thought maybe
he should just cave in and make the kind of music
that his fans seemed to want. But the thought of

doing that crushed his very spirit. It just wasn't who he was.

There was nothing wrong with country music. In fact, he loved it. When given the chance to control any radio, he was inevitably going to change the station to country. But the type of music he wanted to create was a hybrid of sorts, and for that reason he just didn't quite fit into the mold.

Music had always been a huge part of his soul. In fact, he often felt like it was impossible to separate where he ended and the music began.

And lately, not playing his music on a consistent basis had really bothered him. He missed sharing that part of himself with other people.

The funny thing was that he didn't miss being on the road or standing on a stage in front of thousands of adoring fans screaming his name. He didn't even miss the paycheck yet since he was still getting royalties from the music he'd made in recent years.

Laura was on his mind all the time. How would he tell her who he was? Would it change what she thought about him?

This was a woman who loved classical music. Was she going to look down on him for being a country music singer? She'd made it abundantly clear that she didn't like country music, yet when he played for her she was stunned.

He wanted to see that look on her face again.

Scratch that. He wanted to *put* that look on her face again.

Sawyer didn't know why he felt so worried about telling her. Being with her was like a vacation from his former life. This was someone who just thought of him as a regular guy, and he wanted to maintain that as long as he could.

The shop had only been open for a little while, but he'd seen a light in her eyes he hadn't seen previously. She was opening up, making friends in town.

He had taken her over to Jolt to be introduced to Rebecca, and the two of them were already cooking up cross promotional opportunities between them. They seemed to be creating a plan for world domination, he thought to himself. Cupcakes and coffee would soon take over the globe.

Of course, as soon as Laura had walked out of Jolt to take a phone call, Rebecca had pulled Sawyer aside and asked if he might be interested in singing there a couple of nights a week. He told her he'd get back to her on that, and then reminded her not to say anything to Laura about who he was. Singing at Jolt was sure to cause a frenzy that he wasn't ready for at the moment.

When they were out on the streets of January Cove, he would often wear a baseball cap and sunglasses in the hopes that no fans would wander up and start talking to him. So far it had worked, but it was only a matter of time before word got around that he was in town.

Most of the locals could care less. They'd known him since he was a small child, and he wasn't a celebrity to them. There were tourists coming into town every day, though, and somebody was sure to recognize him before too long.

"So, are you enjoying being the owner of a successful cupcake bakery?" he asked her with a smile as they walked down the road to grab a bite of lunch. It was Sunday afternoon, a day that Laura had decided to keep the bakery closed. She needed one day off at least.

"I'm really enjoying it. A lot more than I thought I would. Definitely better than my previous job!"

"Well good. That means that you'll be sticking around in January Cove for a long time then?" he asked with a hopeful smile.

"I think so," she said. "What about you? When are you planning on going back to your regular life in Nashville?"

"I don't know…"

"I would think you'd want to get back soon, especially if you're trying to build your career there. January Cove isn't exactly the place to be if you want to build a music career."

"True. But I've been missing home, and it's been really good to be here." She had no idea that the reason it had been so good was because of her very existence in his small world.

"Vacations are good, but I'm sure that you don't want to waste your talents by working in my bakery for the rest of your life," she said looking at him.

"Oh, it's not so bad," he said with a laugh. "My boss is kind of tough, but I can deal with it."

"Seriously, though, thank you so much for all the help getting the bakery opened. I couldn't have done it without you," she said, placing her hand on his upper arm and squeezing lightly. The small gesture sent shockwaves through his body. He had been touched by a lot of women, mostly fangirls that followed him from concert to concert, but never had he felt like that when a woman had simply touched his arm.

"I wanted to talk to you about something."

"That never sounds good..." she said with a nervous laugh.

"You came to January Cove to live out some of your mother's dreams. When exactly were you planning to get started with that?"

She laughed nervously again. "I was kind of hoping you wouldn't remember that."

"I have a memory like an elephant. What does that mean anyway? Do elephants have particularly good memories? I mean what kind of studies have they done on this?" he said, starting to babble.

"I really don't know. But I'm going to go back to

Addy's house and look that up on Wikipedia..." she said, pretending to turn in the other direction before he grabbed her arm and pulled her back. They stopped, with him looking down into her beautiful green eyes. His throat felt like it was closing up or some kind of enormous lump had formed there.

"Laura, you're just putting this off. Don't you think you need to get started on doing some of these things? And maybe adding in some that you'd like to do for yourself?"

"I don't know. I already came here so that's one of the things off the vision board."

"What about the skydiving and the riding of a motorcycle..."

"There's no way in the world that I'm going to skydive. I don't see any reason to jump out of a perfectly good airplane." She walked over and sat down on a metal bench that was attached to the sidewalk just outside of the dry cleaners. Sawyer joined her, sitting down and leaning against her. Shockingly, she leaned her head and laid it on his shoulder. It was just a friendly thing to do, not anything particularly romantic, but he could've sat there forever.

"It's time for you to start living. Discovering who you really are. And I want to help you," he said softly. She picked up her head, leaving an immediate void on his shoulder.

Turning sideways, she pulled her knee up onto

the bench and faced him. "Sawyer, you've already helped me so much. I mean I met you by hitting you with my car, and yet you've still helped me open a bakery and start a successful business. You've been a great friend, and I will cherish this time we've spent together for the rest of my life. You don't have to put your life on hold to help me with the dreams that my mother had. That's insane."

He turned to face her, pushing a stray hair out of her eyes and could have sworn he felt her jolt when he touched her. Maybe she did feel something for him.

"Quit trying to run me away. I don't want to go back to Nashville, and I might never go back. So let me help you. It will be fun for me, and hopefully fun for you. Can you just trust me to set some things up?"

She sat there, her lips pursed together tightly before a smile finally appeared on her face. She nodded quickly, almost imperceptibly.

"Yes. I do trust you. You haven't done anything to make me mistrust you so far."

His guts wrenched together. She had plenty of reason to mistrust him. She had no idea who he was or what he really did.

"Right. You can trust me. So starting this afternoon, we're going to work on some of those vision board dreams."

"This afternoon? I was thinking maybe a couple of weeks..."

"Oh no! I know you well enough to know that we don't need to delay," he said with a laugh before standing up and holding out his hand to her. "Come on. I've got some things to check into, so I don't have time to sit here on this park bench all day."

"What have I gotten myself into?" she said, taking his hand and standing up. He didn't want to let her hand go, but he did have things to do and right now he had to get back to his house to check a few things on his computer.

She handed him his lone crutch - one that he planned to get rid of soon - and they made their way down the road.

LAURA DIDN'T KNOW what to think. There seemed to be some kind of connection, some kind of chemistry, with Sawyer while they were sitting on the park bench. Maybe she was just overanalyzing things, but she got the distinct impression that he might have similar feelings as hers.

How was this even possible? She had only known him for a couple of weeks now, and he was going back to Nashville at some point. He couldn't stay in January Cove and have the kind of career he deserved.

As much as she was attracted to him, his music had touched her in a way that even classical hadn't. The only way to be a true friend to him was to encourage him to go back to Nashville and not give up. His music needed to be shared with the world.

The truth was she didn't want to open herself up and get hurt by falling in love with someone who had other plans. Ted had had other plans, and it left her in the lurch and lonely as his wife.

Still, there was something about Sawyer that was mysterious. She had moments where she felt like he might be keeping something from her, but then he was so genuine and kind that she couldn't imagine that. She sometimes mentally slapped herself for thinking such a thing.

And now as she sat on the front porch of Addy's Inn, she worried what he was going to get her into this afternoon.

"Ready?" he asked, as he hobbled down the sidewalk. Things had gotten better with his leg over the last few days, so he was only using one crutch now. Sometimes he threw it to the side and attempted to limp his way around places, but he almost always ended up grabbing the crutch again.

"I am. How are we getting there?" she asked, just as a cab pulled up in front of the bed-and-breakfast. "We could've taken my car."

"We couldn't do that and have it be a surprise,

now could we?" he asked with a smile. That dimple was really becoming quite tempting for her.

They loaded into the car and started driving. "Where are we going?" Laura asked after about ten minutes. They were pulling out of the city limits of January Cove and heading up the coastline, but she had no idea where they were headed.

"You really don't understand the definition of surprise, do you?" Sawyer said with a half smile.

"Well I don't like not knowing what's happening."

"Isn't that what you got you into this position in the first place?" Sawyer whispered, so the driver couldn't hear every bit of their conversation.

"I'm not in trouble. I just haven't exactly lived the exciting life most people would enjoy. Maybe I just like quiet. Maybe I'm just an introverted, calm person who wants to live a quiet life."

"Do you believe that? I mean, at your core, right here, do you believe that?" he asked, putting the tips of his fingers over her heart. She felt chills running throughout her body, like one big hot flash from her toes to the top of her head.

"Not really," she said, glancing at him, her voice shaky.

"Sometimes, don't you just want to live on the edge? To feel the blood pumping through your veins? To not have a clue what's about to happen next?"

Their eyes locked for just a moment, and for a

split second she thought he was going to kiss her, but then he cleared his throat and sat back.

They continued riding for another ten minutes before the driver pulled into a parking lot with what looked like some kind of airplane hanger.

They stopped the car, and Sawyer got out, grabbing his one crutch beside him.

"What is this? I told you that I'm not jumping out of an airplane," she said, following him out of the car. The cab pulled away and left them standing there.

Laura was irritated. Had he not listened to her? Was he about to try to force her to do something she didn't want to do?

"Can you just let go and trust me? Just for a minute?" he asked. Before she could respond, the large door of the hangar opened, revealing a helicopter and an older man dressed in a flight suit of some kind.

"Sawyer, what's going on..." she said as he started walking toward the man.

"Sawyer! Long time no see, my boy!" the older man said. He looked like a mixture of Sean Connery and Sam Elliott, and Laura could just imagine the man being the center of every woman's attention at some point in his life.

"Cal! How's it going, old man?" Sawyer said as he embraced the man with a tight hug. It was obvious that this was someone he'd known for a long time and had a great fondness for.

"Oh, I can't complain," Cal said with a bright smile. He was what Laura's mother would have referred to as a "silver fox", with perfectly straight teeth and the kind of graying hair that made women swoon. There wasn't an ounce of fat on him, and he had visible muscles under the military green flight suit he was wearing. "And this is?"

Sawyer put his free arm around Laura's shoulder. "This is my good friend, Laura Bennett. She owns the new Sweetcakes bakery in January Cove."

"Nice to meet you, Cal," Laura said, reaching out and shaking his hand. "How do you two know each other?"

Cal laughed. "Well, I'm a bit old now, but I used to teach this guy how to play guitar."

"Ahhh... Well, you did a fantastic job. Did you teach him to sing too?" Laura asked.

"That would be a no. Cal can't carry a tune in a bucket," Sawyer joked.

"Well, sonny boy, it doesn't look like you can carry much of anything these days yourself. What on Earth did you do?" he asked, pointing at the air cast and crutch.

Sawyer cut his eyes at Laura and then chuckled. "She hit me with her car. That's how we met."

Cal broke into hysterical laughter. "Well, I'd say you know how to make a great entrance, ma'am!"

Laura joined in their laughter. "So, is someone going to tell me why we're here?"

"You'll see," Sawyer said as he nodded toward the helicopter. "First, Cal is going to take us on a little ride."

Laura's stomach knotted up. She wasn't a fan of big airplanes or heights, and a helicopter definitely wasn't on her bucket list. But for some reason, she wanted to trust him.

"Cal used to be in the Air Force back in the day. Now he runs charters all up and down the coast," Sawyer whispered to her as they walked toward the helicopter. "You're safe, Laura." Without a word, he slipped his hand into hers and squeezed, and he didn't let go until they reached the helicopter.

Cal helped them both up into the chopper after he moved it onto the helipad. Sawyer struggled a bit with his air cast, but he seemed intent on not allowing his injury to keep him from doing anything he wanted. She admired his tenacity.

"Ready?" Cal called from the front, yelling through headsets they were both wearing. Laura jumped with surprise when his voice boomed in her ears. Sawyer laughed and took her hand once again, squeezing it. She had no idea what that meant, but she wasn't about to let it go.

The blood was definitely pumping through her body as the aircraft took flight, and Laura had never felt more alive.

CHAPTER 10

She was holding on to his hand like it was a life preserver as the copter lifted off the ground. Her face was turning a pale shade of white at first, but as the scenery came into view, Laura finally loosened her grip and color returned to her cheeks.

Sawyer was having a hard time looking at the ocean views beneath them. He couldn't stop staring at her. Watching her as she looked out the window like a child who'd never seen anything. Her mouth was slightly open, her eyes as wide as he'd seen them. A slight smile on her face, those bee-stung lips that turned upward slightly, forming into the most perfect look of peace he'd ever seen.

But she still didn't release his hand.

Taking her hand had been a calculated decision, although he'd hoped she didn't notice that. He wanted to see what she'd do. Would she pull away? Would she yell at him for being so presumptuous?

"Look at that," she said into the headset, pointing below them at a beautiful, large plantation. The area was full of places like this, hidden gems across the low country landscape of Georgia and South Carolina. Places lost in time with buildings that held a history like no other. Moss covered oaks that formed into shapes that looked like something out of a child's fantasy novel. "So beautiful."

"Yes. Beautiful is the perfect word," he said. He wasn't looking at what she was looking at. He was looking at her, and when she unexpectedly turned and caught him staring, he was sure that he blushed for the first time in his life.

Thankfully, she smiled and turned back to the window. Sawyer stared down at their hands, still intertwined, and noticed how they fit perfectly together. Like they were made for each other.

The chopper started to make its descent landing on a grassy area. Laura, as if on cue, looked at him with furrowed eyebrows.

"Where are we..."

Sawyer reached over and put his index finger over her lips. "Shhh..." he said, using every bit of his willpower not to replace his finger with his own lips. As expected, her lips felt soft and plump at the same time.

Moments later, Cal had helped them disembark

from the helicopter. He watched as Laura looked around in confusion.

"Thanks again, man," Sawyer said to Cal, giving him a quick hug.

"Anytime. Nice to meet you, Laura. Have fun, you two!" Cal said with a wink before climbing back inside the helicopter and lifting off. Laura stared into the sky, shielding her eyes from the hot early afternoon sun as she watched him fly away.

She turned and looked at Sawyer. "Okay. What in the world are we doing here? I feel like Cal just dropped us in the middle of nowhere."

"Come on," he said, waving her toward the other side of the clearing. "Trust…" Laura followed him as he hobbled along. "Take a look."

Sawyer pointed down a small hilly area, and Laura's mouth dropped open. In front of them was a huge amusement park that had just opened a few weeks before and featured one of the South's biggest roller coasters. About half an hour from January Cove by air, the place was busy with tourists who wanted to say they had ridden the Mega Monster Coaster.

"What in the world are we doing here?" she asked with a hesitant smile.

"I think you know."

"You aren't seriously wanting to ride *that* roller coaster over there, are you?"

"Well, sweetcakes," he said, making an obvious

pun about her bakery, "I didn't fly you over here for nothing."

Sawyer reached for her hand as they made their way down the hill. Admittedly, he almost fell down the incline a couple of times while trying to both hold her hand and be the macho alpha male, and not fall on his ass because of the stupid crutch he required at the moment.

"Are you sure you're up for this?" she asked, a hint of sarcasm in her voice as she pointed to his cast.

"Oh, really? You wanna go there? Are you sure *you* are up for this?" he said with a grin.

She paused for a moment and then replied, "Nope. I'm completely and utterly terrified at the moment."

"I've got you, Laura. I promise," he said, holding both of her hands in his and looking down at her. "And when we get back to January Cove, you can check this off your mother's list, okay?"

She nodded quickly and took a deep breath as they approached the line for the coaster.

HE SAID HE HAD HER, and she believed him. For some reason, she believed everything he said to her. Never in her life had she been so completely scared and felt so completely safe at the same time.

Watching Sawyer maneuver around with his air cast and a crutch had been sometimes comical, but always inspiring. Already he had gone further out of his way to take care of her than Ted ever had. It was unfair to compare the two men because there was no comparison to Sawyer.

He was, without a doubt, one-hundred percent Southern gentleman. She'd watched him for days now, noting in her mind all of the ways that he fit the description of "chivalrous". For instance, when they walked on the sidewalk, he would inevitably move to the outside, closest to the road. When she'd asked him why, he explained.

"Southern men are taught to protect women, and by walking on the side closest to the street, we can protect women from cars, mud being splashed... things like that."

Laura had laughed and said, "Someone should've protected you from me."

Even when she drove them places, Sawyer would open her door. When they got to the bakery in the mornings, he would open that one too. She was starting to get so used to having her door opened, that she walked right into a glass door at the local gas station when she was by herself.

"Ticket please," she uninterested male teenager said when they finally made it to the front of the line.

Sawyer handed them the two tickets he'd bought

online, unbeknownst to her. They found a suitable car and climbed in. Laura immediately searched for the seatbelt and anything else that looked like it might strap her in tightly.

"You okay?" Sawyer asked with a laugh when he saw her frantically looking for locks or chains.

"Nope." She really wasn't, and she had no idea why on Earth her demure, calm, level-headed mother would have wanted to ride this kind of Satan-inspired death machine.

As if on cue, Sawyer reached for her hand, as he'd done all day long. She knew it likely meant nothing romantic and was just the gesture of a friend who knew she was scared. And she appreciated it, even if every time he did it she wanted to jump on him and never let go.

Movement. There was movement. Laura fidgeted in her seat as the train of cars started lurching forward. She wanted to bolt, but there was no way out. She was going to die. This was how she was going to die. And when she arrived at the pearly gates, she was going to yell at her mother for making her die in such a stupid way.

"Oh my goshhhhh....." she yelled as the thing catapulted them forward. Sawyer squeezed her hand ever tighter, and she wasn't sure if he was trying to calm her down or calm himself down.

"Woooooo!" she heard people screaming, hands held in the air. No thank you. She would keep her hands to herself. One was holding on to Sawyer, but the other was firmly grasping the fiberglass death chamber she was riding in.

And then something unexpected happened. She looked at Sawyer, and he was laughing and holding up his other hand, and she started to have fun as the coaster whipped up and down and even upside down. Her cheeks hurt from smiling, and there was a distinct possibility that she had swallowed a bug, but she was having fun.

When the ride stopped, her hair was untamable and her eyes were dry, but she was alive. And she felt pride. She was proud that she'd done it, and glad it was over. Without thinking, she turned to Sawyer and hugged his neck, planting a kiss on his cheek.

"Thank you for making me do that," she said softly as the ride attendant began unlocking her seatbelt. Sawyer's mouth opened as if to say something, but they had to get out of the car.

SHE HAD KISSED HIS CHEEK. And he'd had to pinch his own leg to interrupt the thought of just kissing her full on the lips. Of course, that might have embarrassed the adolescent, acne-faced boy who was trying to get them off the ride.

"Now what? I mean, we were dropped off by a helicopter," Laura said with a laugh.

"Well, I thought we could kill two birds with one stone," he said. "But that's a little later. For now, I thought we could hang out here for a bit?"

Laura nodded. The first thing they did was buy some cotton candy. Laura was like a kid, smiling and laughing as she enjoyed the sweet treat.

"You've got a little right there," Sawyer said, taking his finger and catching a stray piece of the pink treat on the corner of Laura's mouth. Without thinking, he licked it off his finger, and Laura seemed surprised.

"So, I remember you saying that you played baseball in high school?"

"Yep. I was a pitcher," he said proudly.

"Well, how would you feel about winning me a stuffed animal?" she asked.

"You don't think I can do it?"

"You know what, Sawyer? I think you can do just about anything."

His heart literally skipped a beat. That was only supposed to happen to girls, right?

"So, if I'm understanding you correctly, I'm basically a hero, right?"

She laughed. "If you can win me that giant teddy bear right there, I'll call you my hero." She pointed to a big brown teddy bear that would require him to knock down five stacks of cans in a row, all with one throw each. If he was honest with himself, there was no way he'd do it. But right now he just wanted to be called her hero, so maybe this would be like the times when mothers lifted cars off their kids because of an adrenaline rush. She certainly had his adrenaline pumping.

"Deal," he said, remembering that he'd just recovered from his shoulder injury and probably shouldn't tell the doctor he'd done this.

"Oh, wait. Your shoulder. I'm so sorry, Sawyer. I wasn't thinking. Don't try this..." she said, reaching out and touching his shoulder.

"I want to be your hero," he whispered as he leaned into her ear. Before he moved away, she whispered back.

"You already are."

"Step right up!" the guy yelled, ruining the moment completely. "You ready to play, mister?"

Laura shook her head at Sawyer.

"Yep. I want to win the pretty lady that big teddy bear right there."

∼

"ARE YOU SURE YOU'RE OKAY?" Laura asked as Sawyer rubbed his shoulder after throwing three balls.

"Yes, Laura. I'm fine. Now, don't mess up my mojo," he said, cutting his eyes at her. He'd already knocked down the first three sets with one shot each. Only two more, and he'd have her bear.

Watching him was riveting to her. The way his

face was so focus and determined. The way his back muscles tightened up and slid underneath the soft gray fabric of his t-shirt. The way his jeans were tight in all the right places, and she could see the muscle in his upper thighs.

"Bam!" the carny yelled when Sawyer knocked down the fourth set of cans.

Laura clapped her hands together and grinned. "You're so good!"

Sawyer smiled. "I'm going to get you that bear." His Southern drawl and deep voice made her legs feel wobbly, so she stabilized herself on the pole that was holding up the overhang over the game area.

And with that, he turned and released the final ball from his hand, smashing the last stack of cans and sending one reeling so far that it bonked the carny right on the head.

"Yay! I'm so proud of you!" Laura shouted as she hugged him tightly around the neck. She could feel him stabilizing himself so as not to fall, so she started to pull away but he reached around and grabbed her waist tightly, his face buried in the crook of her neck. The feel of his mouth on her skin sent another hot flash throughout her body.

"You're worth it," he whispered, his lips against her ear now. She pulled back a bit and went to kiss him on the cheek, but instead he turned his head unexpectedly and she ended up brushing his lips with hers.

And it was heaven. Just for a moment, his lips were touching her lips and everything was right in the world. She wanted to stay there, but the shock of it caused them both to stop and pull back for a moment, and that was just enough time for the carny to push the giant teddy bear between them.

"Congrats, man! I've never seen anybody slay this game like that!" he said. The guy had blond dreadlocks and more tattoos than Laura thought was possible, but his accent was that of a California surfer. "Hey... Aren't you Sawyer Griffin?"

Laura watched as Sawyer quickly pulled his baseball cap down further and nervously shuffled his feet.

"You *are* Sawyer Griffin!" the guy said before Sawyer could answer. "Man, I heard you play in Nashville about two years ago..."

"Really? Cool. Listen, I'm kind of in a hurry here, but thanks so much for the game." Sawyer quickly - well, as quickly as an air cast would allow - whisked Laura away from the game booth. She was now carrying the bear, which was about half her size.

"What was that about?"

"Oh, he probably saw me in a club or something. I told you I've been trying to make it in Nashville for a long time now."

She stopped and waited for him to notice.

"What?" he said, turning around.

"I wasn't referring to the fact that he noticed you. I mean why did you seem so nervous about it?"

Sawyer sighed and took a step toward her. "Look, I don't want to have to explain that I'm a big, fat failure to the guy, okay?"

She tilted her head and looked up at him. "You definitely aren't a failure to me, Sawyer Griffin. You're my hero," she said, raising the bear up beside her face and smiling.

And with that, she rose up onto her tiptoes and kissed him on that dimple she'd been staring at for so many days.

THE AFTERNOON SUN started to tuck itself away behind the orange and yellow streaks of the sky, and Sawyer couldn't remember a time he'd been more at ease. Peaceful. Calm. Serene.

As they walked out of the amusement park, she turned and looked at him. "You're not a failure, you know."

"Oh really?"

"You're a true musical genius, Sawyer. And if Nashville can't see it, then I don't ever want to go there."

"Boycotting Nashville?" he asked with a smile.

"If I need to," she said. "So where are we going

now? Because I have this gigantic bear that needs a ride."

"Well, that is a bit of a problem," he said, scrunching up his nose.

"Why?"

"Because our ride doesn't really have room for him." Sawyer pointed a few feet over to a motorcycle that was parked next to a light pole.

"What?" Laura's eyes were wide. "Come on, Sawyer. I'm all for taking risks, but you can't drive that thing with a boot on your foot."

"You're right. I can't. But you can."

"What? Are you insane? I can't drive a motorcycle! I can barely ride a bike!"

"Well, now, that's just sad. One thing at a time. Once I'm all healed up, I'd be glad to take you for a ride." He winked at her.

"Ew. Don't be *that* guy," she said, laughing.

"You're right. Sorry. Anyway, back to our little problem here. I'm going to need you to drive this thing. I've done it a million times, so I'll tell you what to do."

Laura stared at him for a moment and then sighed. "Fine. But what do we do about my new friend here?"

"I can get some rope to tie him down behind me..." Sawyer started looking around for a source of rope, which made Laura laugh.

"Well, unless there's a rope fairy, I don't think that's a viable option."

"We don't need to ride far to get to our next destination."

"You mean there's more?" she asked. "I'm a little scared."

"Let's just call another cab. I don't want you to lose Mr. Bear here," Sawyer said, pulling out his cell phone. Laura looked to her side and then turned back to Sawyer, grinning.

"Would it hurt your feelings if I gave him away?"

"But you love him."

"I do, and I'll never forget you winning him for me. But look." She pointed to a little girl, maybe eight or nine years old, who was in a wheelchair. Her family had just finished trying to win her something, and Laura had seen them earlier in the park. She noticed them leaving empty handed.

"You're a special person, Laura Bennett."

Laura walked over to the family. "Hi. I was wondering if you could help me with something?"

"With what?" the little girl asked.

"Well, my friend here won me this wonderfully large bear, but we're riding on that motorcycle. This poor guy won't fit on there with us."

The little girl's eyes lit up when Laura handed the stuffed animal over. "Really? I can keep him?"

"You'd be doing me a huge favor if you would," Laura said with a smile.

"Does he have a name?" the little girl asked.

Sawyer suddenly piped in. "His name is Sweetcakes."

The little girl grinned from ear to ear as her parents wheeled her to their car. Before Laura could turn around, Sawyer wrapped his arms around her from behind and whispered in her ear. "Now, you're my hero."

SAWYER COULDN'T BELIEVE he'd talked her into riding the motorcycle, but there she stood - ready and willing to try it. They had to go about twenty miles or so before their next destination, so he thought she could do it.

"Okay, safety first," he said, pulling the helmets off the back and helping Laura get hers on before putting on his own. Laura had a backpack, and he was able to store it in a compartment on the back. "And gloves," he said, handing them to her. She slipped them on, and he had to admit it was a sexy thing to watch.

"Next?"

"Okay, so this is the clutch here. And this is your foot peg. This right here is the shifter..." he started. After going over all of the parts and pieces, and showing her how to start the bike, she climbed on. Just seeing her sitting on the bike with those black leather gloves did things to him that he hoped she didn't notice.

"What's this again?" she asked, a bit of nervousness apparent in her voice.

"That's your front break lever, and this is the throttle right here," he said, leaning forward enough that he could smell her perfume, and that was doing things to him. "You... um... get most of your breaking capabilities from your front brakes... in case you didn't know."

"Yeah, Sawyer. I totally knew that," she said with a sarcastic smile.

"Right. Yeah. So, okay. Let's give it a try," he said, climbing on the bike behind her. He stabilized them before telling her to put the kickstand up. Sawyer reached around and started the bike until it was idling. "Ready?"

"I don't want to hurt you," she said, worried that she would wreck the bike.

"I trust you, Laura."

"Well, I'm glad one of us does," she said with a shaky laugh.

CHAPTER 11

*L*aura couldn't believe the day she'd had so far. Now, as she sped down the highway on a motorcycle at sunset, she felt like she was in a dream.

For the first few miles, she'd been terrified. But with Sawyer giving her commands in her ear, she had managed to not kill or maim either one of them yet.

Traffic was light since it was Sunday, and the view of the ocean as they breezed down the highway was breathtaking. But more than that, the feel of Sawyer holding on to her from behind was something she never wanted to forget.

His hands were strong, and his grip on her was firm. He trusted her, literally with his life. He believed in her. He had shown her in so many different ways that she was capable of doing anything she set her mind to. And now she wanted to do it all.

"Turn here," he said as they approached a parking lot. She slowly turned in and came to a stop, being careful to put down the kickstand so they didn't topple over.

"What is this place?"

"Well, hopefully it's our next ride, if all went according to plan," he said with a sly smile.

"What about the bike?"

"Someone will be along to pick it up shortly."

"Oh my gosh!" Laura said. "Your crutch. We left it back at the amusement park..."

Sawyer laughed. "Are you just now noticing that?"

Laura shrugged her shoulders. "In my defense, I was trying to not kill us at the time."

"When I learned I was a hero, I dropped that crutch like a bad habit," he said, leaning against a wooden support near a small dock at the water's edge. "Kind of regretting that now, though. My leg is pretty stiff."

"Here. Sit down for a minute," Laura said, helping him down onto a tall tree stump that was at the edge of the parking lot. "Does this help?" she asked as she rubbed the top of his leg carefully.

Sawyer looked away and sighed. "More than you know."

At first, she thought he was being "that guy"

again, but he seemed to truly be trying to restrain himself. She continued rubbing his leg until he suddenly stood up and almost lost his balance in the process.

"What are you doing, crazy man?" she said.

"Look, I don't know how else to say this, but if you don't stop rubbing my leg like that then I might not be able to stop myself from..."

"From what?" she asked softly, looking up at him. His eyes connected with hers.

"From this," he said, pulling her as close as he could and kissing her hard on the mouth. His kiss was intense, almost frantic, but then it softened and became the most sensual thing she'd ever felt in her life. His tongue found hers, and they fit together perfectly, like her lips had been made to dance with his.

His hands held her head in place, his fingers weaving in and out of her hair until they came around and held her cheeks. He pulled back and looked at her, breathless and laughing.

"I'm so sorry, Laura. I shouldn't have assumed... But I couldn't help it... But that's no excuse..."

"Sawyer?"

"Yeah?"

"Shut up," she said before pulling him back toward her and kissing him until the sun officially went down.

SAWYER LEANED against the railing of the small dock, completely aware that time had gotten away from him. The night wasn't supposed to end with an hour's worth of making out in the middle of nowhere without a ride home, but it did, and it was perfect.

Laura leaned against his shoulder, her eyes closed as they listened to the waves crashing into shore over and over again.

"So what were we going to do?" Laura asked. "I mean before we got carried away?"

Sawyer chuckled and kissed the top of her head softly. "Well, see that jet ski down there? We were going to ride it to the ferry at January Cove."

"Oops."

"Hey, given the choice between riding a jet ski and kissing you, I'd have chosen the latter every day for the rest of my life," he said softly. She snuggled in closer to his chest.

"So when do you think Brad will be here?"

"Should be any time now."

"Thank God he was available," she said.

Brad pulled up moments later and got out of his truck with a cocky grin on his face.

"Come on, love birds," he said.

Sawyer and Laura cleared their throats simultaneously, both uncomfortable with his terminology.

"Thanks for picking us up, man," Sawyer said as he limped to the truck and helped Laura inside.

"Dude, where are your crutches?"

"I tossed my crutch away at the amusement park," Sawyer said. "Tough guys don't use crutches."

"Okay, tough guy, let me help you into the truck," Brad teased as Sawyer held onto him for stability.

"Shut up."

~

BRAD HAD TAKEN Laura back to Addy's before driving Sawyer around the corner to his house. He'd wanted a big goodbye kissing scene, but having Brad there wasn't exactly conducive to romance.

"So, it looks like things are getting pretty hot and heavy with you and Laura, huh?" Brad said, pulling a beer from Sawyer's almost empty refrigerator. Such was the life of a bachelor, he thought to himself.

"I don't know where it's going, but yeah, tonight was pretty epic," Sawyer said, immediately regretting his choice of trying to use trendy words. Brad slid another beer across the kitchen counter that he leaned against while Sawyer lowered himself onto one of the bar stools.

"Man, when are you going to be honest with her? I'm surprised no one around here has blown your cover yet."

Sawyer took a long sip of his beer and then

hung his head. "I'm afraid I've waited too long. I wasn't expecting things to get so... intense... today. And now I feel terrible for lying to her about who I am."

"You know the tourists are already coming into town, Sawyer. You're going to get recognized, especially helping her at the bakery."

Sawyer sighed. "Soon. I'll tell her soon."

"Good. I hope you do."

"I just hope she understands."

LAURA SAT AT JOLT, having a nice cup of coffee, after a long first half of the day at the bakery. Sawyer had gone to rehab alone, finally able to get himself there without her driving him.

She had come to work wondering if things would be awkward after their kissing marathon the night before, but it wasn't. He was just as easygoing and interested in her as he had been, but there had been no more kissing with customers constantly milling around.

Of course, they'd spent the day making what her mother would've called "goo goo eyes" at each other. Laura remembered back to middle school when she'd had her first "boyfriend" - Tyler Dillard. They had also made goo goo eyes at each other. He was a sweet kid, but he got to be a little too much for her when he kept sticking love poems he wrote into her locker.

"Long day?" Rebecca asked as she approached Laura's table, knocking her out of her walk down memory lane.

"So far. But good," Laura said with a smile. She took a sip of her iced coffee as Rebecca sat down.

"Yeah, it gets busier this time of the year with all of the tourists starting to check out our little hidden paradise."

"It definitely is a paradise," Laura said. "I didn't think I'd love it here so much. Or so soon." She really hadn't planned to like January Cove at all, given that it wasn't on her dream board. Actually, she didn't even have a dream board yet.

"Coming from New York City, I thought I'd get bored here. It was an adjustment not to hear the noises I was used to like police sirens and honking horns. But I quickly adapted, and now this is a home I could never leave." Laura nodded and drank more of her coffee, noting that she only had a few more minutes before she had to re-open for the afternoon crowd.

"Yeah, Baltimore was much the same. I thought I'd struggle going from a big city lifestyle to such a quiet place, but I feel peaceful here. More peaceful than I think I've ever felt in my life."

"Well, good. That means I might have your awesome cupcakes for years to come then," Rebecca said with a wink before she stood up to help a new customer who had just walked through the door. Laura waved goodbye as she picked up what was left of her drink and hurried toward Sweetcakes.

~

"QUICK! Lock the door before another person gets in," Laura said laughing as Sawyer turned the lock and switched the sign to "closed".

As thankful as she was for such loyal customers, the day had been busier than she expected. Before long, she'd have to hire some help. Sawyer wasn't going to work there forever, and she didn't expect him to. His talents would be wasted.

"Wow! I don't think we've ever had so many people in here before," Sawyer said, wiping real sweat off his forehead. "I guess tourist season has officially arrived."

"I guess so." She smiled nervously at him, wondering what to say now that they were completely alone. It would take another half hour to clean and close up.

"Listen, I need to talk to you about something..." he said, wiping his hands on his apron.

Uh oh. That was never a good sentence to hear from a man, she thought. He was regretting their impulsive kissing extravaganza.

"Okay," she said softly, trying not to make eye contact.

"Remember how your mom had that one thing on her vision board about dating a younger man?"

Okay, that was a weird way to start. "Um… yeah…"

"Well, I was wondering if you'd like to do that?"

"Sawyer! What in the world is wrong with you? You're going to fix me up with some young buck just so I can check something off my mother's vision board?" She couldn't believe what she was hearing.

Sawyer smiled slyly and removed his wallet from his back pocket. "I might look wiser and older, Laura, but remember I'm six months *younger* than you." He held out his license, and Laura leaned over to look at it, a confused look on her face.

"Sawyer, are you asking me on a real date?" she asked, smiling bigger than she intended to.

He slipped his wallet back into his pocket and walked forward, putting his hands on her waist. "Well, since that's the only way I might get more of these lips," he said, leaning in and brushing his against hers lightly, "then I guess I'd better be."

Laura sucked in a deep breath when he pulled away and looked at her, sad at the absence of his lips. "What are you proposing we do on this date?"

Sawyer leaned against the bar that ran down the side of the bakery. "Well, I propose that you be my plus one at my high school reunion tonight at the pier."

Her mouth dropped open. "Tonight? Why didn't you say something earlier?"

"Because I didn't think I was going until Brad started blowing up my phone around lunch time today. He threatened me with bodily harm if I didn't come."

"And you're scared of Brad?" she asked with a laugh as she went back to wiping down the counters.

"Not really, but I was scared he'd keep talking until my ears bled so I gave in. So, what do you say, Miss Bennett? Care to hear lots of silly stories about what an idiot teenage boy I was back in the day?" he asked, his hands in the prayer position.

"Well… I guess it would allow me to check one more thing off my list without having to go over to the local college and search for a hot young guy…"

"Are you saying I'm not a hot young guy?" he asked with a sexy grin.

"No comment."

SAWYER PACED - AS WELL as he could pace with an air cast - in front of Addy's. Addy and Clay were already down at the pier since Adele was watching Anna Grace for the night. Right now, he was waiting for

Laura. Normally, he'd walk up to the door, but the stupid cast made everything more difficult.

He'd been thinking all day about how much of a risk he was taking. What if someone told her who he was? Mentioned one of his albums or concerts? He'd done his best to keep a lid on who he was, and he wanted to tell her in his own way and in his own time, but he could feel time ticking away like a bomb about to go off.

"Wow," he said when she appeared on the front porch. She was wearing a small red sundress that clung to all the right places and a pair of silver sandals. "You look amazing."

He thought she blushed a bit, a smile spreading across her face. "Thank you."

She met him on the sidewalk, and he leaned in to kiss her softly on the cheek. "Are you sure you're ready to go out with a younger man? Think you can keep up?"

She laughed as she looked down at his air cast. "I think so. I'm pretty spry for my age."

"You know what? I refuse to wear this ugly thing on a date with such a beautiful woman," he said, reaching down and popping the cast off his leg. He tossed it behind a bush in front of Addy's.

"Sawyer! Put that back on. You're going to be in pain all night!"

Sawyer slid his arms around her waist and

pressed his lips against her ear. "Not possible. I couldn't possibly be in pain when I look at you."

She smiled at him, and a part of him ached as he thought about lying to her. He could only hope that she would understand why he did it, why he had hidden that part of himself from her for so long. And if she didn't forgive him? He just couldn't think about that right now.

THE PIER WAS all set for Sawyer's reunion, with candles adorning small bistro tables scattered around the old wooden structure. Music was playing softly in the background, the ocean waves adding a special accompaniment to the sounds of pop love songs.

A few couples were already slow dancing, including Addy and Clay, and most everyone else was standing around talking. Sawyer had told her that he didn't know why they were having a reunion since most of these people saw each other everyday in January Cove, but any excuse to get together and have a party was a good one.

Sawyer had struggled a bit to walk there without his cast, but Laura had pretended not to notice. Instead she focused on how good he looked. He was wearing tan shorts and a baby blue t-shirt that showed off his natural tan. His stubble was gone in favor of a freshly shaved look that she loved just as much, and the scent of his cologne was making her want to do things that she'd get arrested for in public.

"So you're Laura Bennett? I've heard all about your delicious cupcakes," Ronni said. "I can't wait to try one!"

"Come on by," Laura said. "Try the hot fudge cupcake. It's my new favorite… this week!" she said with a laugh.

"Ronni is Brad's girlfriend," Sawyer said, explaining who the beautiful leggy blond was. Laura normally steered clear of women who made her feel matronly, but Ronni seemed like a very nice person. So far, everyone in January Cove seemed nice, actually.

"That must be… interesting," Laura said, referring to dating Brad. Ronni giggled.

"It takes a special woman to handle me," Brad said, sneaking up behind Ronni and kissing her on the back of her neck.

"Medication?" Sawyer suggested as the reason she was able to put up with Brad's crazy personality.

"Thinking about it," she whispered loudly.

Laura enjoyed walking around and meeting more people who knew Sawyer when he was a kid. Stories of football games and Homecoming parades and old girlfriends kept her entertained for hours with people she either didn't know or barely knew. She felt at home in a place she'd never visited before a few weeks ago, and these people were already starting to feel like family.

"Are you bored yet?" Sawyer whispered to her as they swayed on the dance floor to *The Way You Look Tonight*. She felt so safe and comfortable in his arms, something she couldn't recall ever feeling with Ted. He slow danced like a bird with a broken wing. And foot.

She looked up at him. "Not at all."

"Good, because I might just stand here holding you in my arms until tomorrow morning, music or not."

That sounded like perfection to her.

WHEN THE REUNION was over and everyone else had left, Laura found herself still snuggled into Sawyer's arms, sitting at the edge of the ocean, the tips of the waves lapping at their feet.

"We should probably go home soon," Sawyer whispered. "We have to open in a few hours." He didn't move, and neither did she.

"I don't want to leave. I think we should just stay here for a few more hours and let people get their own cupcakes."

Sawyer laughed. "Sounds like a plan to me."

Laura breathed in the salty ocean air. This place -

and this man - were making her do things she would never normally do. For a moment, she tried to imagine who she was just a few weeks ago in Baltimore. Sad. Broken. Lonely. Working a job she hated. Missing her mother.

She didn't even feel like the same person anymore.

"Sawyer?"

"Umhmm…" he mumbled against her ear.

"You said once that I need to have my own vision board."

"I remember."

"Well, I have something I want to do as my first thing on my vision board."

"Oh yeah? And what is that?" he asked, curious as he pulled away and looked at her. She grinned.

"Well… have you ever… um… skinny dipped?" She could feel a blush spreading across her face and hoped the darkness would keep him from noticing.

Sawyer cleared his throat and laughed nervously. "Well, believe it or not, I haven't. Lots of my friends did it when we were in school, but I never did."

"Why?"

"I have no idea, honestly."

"Well? Would you like to join me?" she asked, standing up and hoping that she wasn't about to do this alone.

Sawyer stood. "Are you sure about this, Laura?"

"I'm sure. I want to have some experiences,

Sawyer. My *own* experiences. I love my mother, but it's time for me to live. And I don't ever want to ride a roller coaster again."

He took her hands in his and smiled. "Then I will come along for *any* experiences you invite me to. Especially ones that involve you without clothes on."

Laura lightly slapped his shoulder. "You're bad."

"Um, I'm not the one who suggested skinny dipping in the ocean at midnight."

Without a word, Laura summoned her courage and flung her dress over her head, running toward the water in her bra and panties. Sawyer followed quickly behind dropping articles of clothing as he went. Before they made it into the water, every piece of clothing they had between them was scattered around the beach, and Laura had never felt more alive.

AFTER ANOTHER LONG day at work, Laura sat in the chair by the bed with her journal in her lap. She smiled as she thought back over her days with Sawyer. He'd made her do things she would've never done on her own, but now everything in the world seemed possible to her.

But mostly she just reflected on the kissing. Yep. The kissing was the best part. And a few things that happened after the kissing... and after the skinny dipping.

"Laura?" Addy said from the other side of the door.

Laura stood and walked to the door. She opened it expecting to see Addy standing there in her bright pink pajamas, as she was usually wearing by this time of night. Instead, she saw Addy standing with someone else - Carrie.

"Oh my gosh! Carrie! What are you doing here?" Laura squealed as she pulled her friend into a tight embrace. "Oh, sorry, Addy. Is Anna Grace asleep?" Laura asked in a loud whisper.

"No, she's spending the night with my mother while she's in town, actually. You two have fun catching up. Clay and I are going for a late dinner at The Wharf," she said. Laura then noticed she was wearing a tight black dress and heels.

Laura dragged Carrie into her room by her arm. She grabbed the suitcase from Carrie's hand and slid it beside the bed.

"I can't believe you're standing here! I've missed you a ton!" She pulled Carrie into a breath-stopping hug again before finally letting her go.

Carrie grinned. "Well, I had to come see what this January Cove place was all about. And meet the infamous singing stud!"

"You're funny," Laura said, a sly smile spreading

across her face. Then it turned into a full grin as she sat down on the edge of the bed.

"Oh man, something happened! Did you do the deed with the sexy country guy already?" Carrie asked, plopping down on the bed next to her.

"Of course not! You know I'm not that kind of woman!"

"Sexual? I would certainly hope you're that type of woman," Carrie said with a laugh.

"We just met each other, Carrie. I'm not ready for that yet. But, yes, something did happen." She was swooning like a lovesick schoolgirl.

"What? Give me the info, girlfriend!"

Laura spent the next few minutes recounting the whole day at the amusement park and on the motorcycle while Carrie sat with her mouth hanging open.

"So he took you on a rollercoaster - something I've been trying to do since we were in middle school - and on a motorcycle? And he got you to drive it?"

"Yep. Can you believe that?"

"No. No, I cannot."

"And then, we kissed."

"Like a little peck or like an R-rated movie?"

"R-rated movie, for sure. It was… magical," Laura said, her face turning all shades of red as she closed her eyes and sighed. "And then there was last night."

"Last night?"

"He took me to his high school reunion. We

kissed and we danced and we snuggled on the beach after everyone left. And then I asked him to do something with me."

"What? Don't leave me hanging!"

"I asked him to skinny dip."

"You did not!"

"I did too! And it was amazing, Carrie. Skin on skin at midnight in the ocean. I can't even describe how I felt out there. He's so kind and gorgeous and strong."

"You're not even the same person," Carrie said, eying her friend carefully. Laura opened her eyes to find Carrie smiling proudly.

"Of course I am!"

"No. I meant that in a good way, Laura," she said softly. "This guy has done what I could never do. He's brought the old Laura back, but an even better version. Somehow, he's made you believe in yourself again. I saw Sweetcakes when I was being dropped off. It looks amazing!"

Laura knew she was right. In the short time she'd known Sawyer, he'd changed her world. Changed how she felt about herself and what she could accomplish. Made her smile again - a lot.

"I can't wait to meet him," Carrie said.

"Me either! You're going to love him."

"The question is - do you?"

Laura stared at her friend. It was impossible to love someone she'd just met. Wasn't it?

CHAPTER 12

Sawyer leaned back on his sofa and took a deep breath. Today had to be the day. He couldn't keep doing this, keeping up the charade that he was some down on his luck, struggling musician. If Laura even watched a TV entertainment show, she'd find out. If the wrong social media story passed on her newsfeed, she'd know. And he had to be the one to tell her.

Two nights ago, as he held her in his arms on the beach, he knew. She was the one. The only one. There was no going back. Swimming in the ocean naked with this amazing woman had been the highlight of his life.

He'd changed. She'd changed. And somehow they had become perfect for each other in the process.

The ringing of his phone knocked him out of his deep thoughts. "Hello?"

"Man, you're hard to get a hold of lately!" his former agent, Dan, said.

"I've been busy. What do you want?" Sawyer closed his eyes, ready for the onslaught that was sure to come since he hadn't returned to Nashville yet.

"I've got some good news, Sawyer. You know how they say when God closes a door, he opens a window. Well, you've got a big huge window open for you!"

"Dan, have you been drinking? What the heck are you even talking about?"

"Barnwell called. He wants to sign you to his label and immediately drop an album. They even want a U.S. tour planned, and maybe an international one if that one goes well."

"I told you I'm done."

"Don't be a fool, Sawyer. Barnwell will produce the music you want. Think of all the years you put into this! Nobody walks away from something like this. You'll be kicking yourself when you're eighty."

For a moment, Sawyer daydreamed about sitting with Laura in rocking chairs on the front porch of their own beach house, each of them in their eighties. He couldn't imagine regretting anything.

"No. I'm happy here, Dan. I got my life back. I met someone…"

"Oh Good Lord! This is about a woman? I can get you another woman in Nashville who will suit you just as good!"

"Goodbye, Dan." Sawyer ended the call before his anger got the best of him. No woman would suit him like Laura, and he had to tell her the truth. Today.

❧

"So glad you could help me today. Sawyer had a check up with his orthopedic doctor. I don't think the doctor is going to like the fact that he just threw his air cast in the bushes the other night," Laura said laughing.

"Well, this has been fun. Everyone here seems so nice!"

"They are, Carrie. The best people I've ever met."

"So this is home now?" she asked.

Laura stopped for a moment and smiled, before she went back to wiping down the bar. "Yes. This is home now."

"I've never seen you so happy, my friend. I'm proud of you." Carrie pulled Laura into a tight hug. "And your mother would be too."

"And what about Aunt Dahlia?"

"Oh, she's going to love this place! You have to invite her soon."

"I will. I'll email her tonight, in fact. Maybe she can come visit before you leave."

"Oh, sweetie, I can't stay long. I've got to get back to life in the big city."

Laura frowned. "Well, you just remember that

January Cove welcomes everyone, so when you get tired of the noise and the lack of hunky Southern men, you come back and stay, okay?"

Carrie nodded. "Maybe you should work for the tourism department here."

"Hey, you want to go grab a coffee at Jolt?"

"Sure. I need a jolt right now." Carrie said. "My boss is a beast!"

The two women laughed as they locked up and started heading toward the coffee shop. Laura pointed out all of the points of interest in town as they made their way to Rebecca's coffee shop.

"Whoa. Oh. My. God." Carrie stopped in her tracks, her hand over her mouth.

"What?" Laura asked, immediately worried something was majorly wrong with her friend. She turned to see what Carrie was looking at. There was Sawyer at the end of the road, walking toward them but looking down at his phone.

"Sawyer Griffin." Carrie started fanning herself.

"You know him?" Laura was completely confused.

Carrie turned to her friend and then back to Sawyer, who had walked into Jolt ahead of them, still unaware of their presence. A look of recognition spread across her face as she put two and two together.

"That's *your* Sawyer?" she asked.

Laura stared at her friend. "I don't get it. What's going on, Carrie? How do you know Sawyer?"

Carrie took a deep breath. "Did he not tell you who he is?"

"Who he is? I don't even know what that means."

"Laura, Sawyer Griffin is just about one of the biggest stars in country music. He's toured all over the world, and he's produced several albums. I have a ton of his music on my playlist. Look." She handed her phone to Laura, a list of Sawyer's songs taking up the whole page.

Laura stared down at the electronic device as if it was from another planet. She hit play on one of the songs, and sure enough, it was Sawyer. The very same Sawyer who had sung to her in his living room. The same one who told her he was a struggling - and failing - music artist.

"I don't understand..." she stammered. "Why would he do this? Why would he tell me he wasn't successful? He lied to me."

Just then, Sawyer came out of Jolt and noticed Laura standing there with Carrie. A smile spread across his face as he waved at her.

"Hey, beautiful," he said as he leaned in and kissed her cheek. She stilled and didn't make eye contact with him. "Hi. I'm Sawyer. You must be Carrie?" The nervousness in his voice was apparent. He reached out to shake Carrie's hand, but never took his eyes off of Laura.

Carrie slowly nodded, unsure of how to respond. "Yes. Nice to meet you."

"I have to go," Laura said as she started quickly walking back toward the B&B. Sawyer started to chase after her, but Carrie grabbed his arm.

~

"IS SHE OKAY?" he asked.

"No. She's not."

He looked at her, his eyebrows furrowed. "Then I should go catch up with her."

Carrie held on to his arm. "I liked your last album, Sawyer. And I saw you in Baltimore a couple of years ago."

His eyes grew wide. "She knows." It wasn't a question. It was more of a statement. "Damn it. I was going to tell her tonight."

"Well, I think you might be a little late on that one."

"I didn't intend to deceive her, Carrie." He leaned against the brick wall of the old building. "It was just nice being with someone who didn't care who I was."

"She opened herself up to you, Sawyer. And yet again, a man wasn't who he said he was."

"You've known her since you were both kids. Do you think she'll forgive me?"

Carrie bit her lips. "I don't know this new Laura.

She became someone else because of you. I can't say what she'll do, but good luck to you, Sawyer. I think you're going to need it."

~

"KNOCK KNOCK," Carrie said as she slowly entered Laura's room. Laura was standing in the window, looking down on the quiet January Cove streets.

"I feel like a fool."

Carrie hugged her friend from behind. "Sweetie, you couldn't have known. You're not a fan of country music, after all. Now, if he'd been some kind of classical music star…" Carrie's efforts at making a joke fell flat.

"I don't understand why he lied to me. I opened myself up to him in a way that I'd never done with anyone."

"Maybe he has an explanation, Laura. I think he's a good guy…"

"Don't. Do not defend him!" She pulled away from Carrie. "I need some time alone. I'll be back in awhile, okay?"

Before Carrie could answer, Laura was out the door.

~

THE NEXT FEW days were awkward to say the least. Carrie left for Baltimore, and Laura didn't want Sawyer in the bakery. So she worked alone, and it was hard. She put out an ad in the local paper to find some part-time help before she keeled over of exhaustion.

Living in a small town meant seeing Sawyer on the street almost daily. He tried to wave, tried to smile. She would walk the other way even if it meant going the long way. And everyone knew what had happened. She could see it on their faces.

He kept texting her and calling her. She'd hit "ignore" so many times on her phone that she feared she would develop a callus on her thumb. And when he'd shown up at Addy's, Laura had locked her door and refused to answer.

She felt deceived. Everyone around her had known, and yet no one had said a word. Even Addy. And Clay. And Brad.

Maybe she'd been wrong about everyone. Maybe she should go back to Baltimore where she was bored, but at least she knew where people stood. Where their loyalties were. She was an outsider in January Cove, and maybe she would never be part of the crowd.

"Hi, Laura," Addy said softly as she approached the counter in the empty bakery.

"Hello." Laura tried not to make eye contact. "What can I get you?"

"I'd like a red velvet please," she said. "And the opportunity to apologize."

For some reason, Laura couldn't help tearing up. She quickly wiped away the stray tear and pulled a red velvet cupcake from the case, placing it in a clear plastic box and handing it to Addy.

"No apology necessary," she said. "Your loyalty should be with your friend."

Addy handed her the money. "Laura, it wasn't like that. Sawyer had his reasons, and he promised me he would tell you soon and..."

"Addy, I appreciate your hospitality, but I think I should tell you that I've found a rental home over near Savannah. So I'll be moving out this weekend."

Addy looked stunned. "Oh. Okay. Savannah? That's quite a drive..."

"I've got some decisions to make. I'm looking at space over in Savannah. Maybe I'll have someone take over this location. I didn't plan to expand so soon, but life throws you curveballs sometimes."

Addy nodded and took her cupcake. "If I can help you in any way, Laura, please know I'm here. You're a part of January Cove now, and no one wants to see you leave."

"Well, small town life might not be for me, as it turns out." Her gaze followed Sawyer walking down the sidewalk in front of the bakery.

∽

LAURA LOCKED the door to the bakery and looked around, trying to make sure that Sawyer wasn't anywhere to be seen. She hadn't seen him for a couple of days, so maybe he had gone back to Nashville.

Her rental house had gotten delayed. Something about a roof leak. So she would be at Addy's for at least another week.

Instead of going back to her room, she decided to take a walk down to the beach to clear her head. No matter how hard she tried, she couldn't shake the feeling of betrayal.

A part of her felt like she was overreacting. After all, Sawyer hadn't slept with another woman or hidden a secret wife and kids somewhere. At least not that she knew of.

But he had lied. At least by omission. He had let her believe he was just some guy trying to make it in Nashville.

She had felt the worst when she checked his name on Google, which she should have done before. Pages upon pages came up along with videos of his concerts. She had listened to each of his albums, noting how the most recent one was so different, so much more like what he'd played for her that night at his house.

And if she was honest with herself, she missed him. Ached for his presence. How had she fallen so hard and so fast for someone she really didn't know?

That thought scared her, and it made her lose trust in herself a little bit.

Maybe she hadn't changed at all.

She sat down by the water's edge, dipping her now bare feet in the lapping waves. The sun would be going down soon, and something about sitting by the ocean in the dark allowed her to block out all of the voices debating what to do inside of her head.

"You're a hard lady to reach."

Sawyer.

"Go away," she said, too tired to stand up after manning the bakery alone for days.

"No." He sat down beside her and stared out at the open water. "I remember when I was a kid and my father would drive me crazy about something. I always came out here and felt like I could throw my problems to the ocean wind and they'd be magically wiped away."

"And did it work?" she asked softly without looking at him.

"Not once." Sawyer sighed. "Laura, I'm so sorry. I should've told you who I was."

"Yes, you should have."

"I want to explain…"

"And I don't want to hear it. Please just leave me alone, Sawyer."

"I can't do that. I need you to know why I did what I did."

She turned and looked at him, trying desperately

not to show the pain in her face. He looked tired; no less handsome, but tired.

"It doesn't matter," she said softly. "You didn't trust me with who you really are."

His jaw tightened as he sucked in a sharp breath. "See? That's exactly why I didn't tell you," he said, standing up and pacing along the shoreline. She stood to face him.

"What?"

"I've got millions of fans, Laura. Millions. Random strangers want me to sign stuff in case it might be worth money one day. Women throw under garments at me while I'm on stage. When I walk through a crowd, I get pinched on my butt by complete strangers. Does that seem normal to you?"

"Am I supposed to feel sorry for you, Sawyer? You chose the life of a famous musician. Isn't that what you wanted?"

He shook his head and looked down. "I thought you knew me better than this."

"You didn't tell me..."

"No. I didn't. And you want to know why? Because I came back to January Cove to find myself again. People here don't care who I am. They don't follow me around with a camera, waiting for me to look ugly or kiss a woman so they can sell the photo to the tabloids. They don't write nasty blog posts and articles about how sucky my last album was... you know, the one that I poured my heart and soul into? They just accept me as Sawyer. And when I met you and realized you had no idea who I was, it made me happy. You liked me for just being me. Not rich and famous me. Just me. Or so I thought." He sighed. "You said I didn't trust you with who I really was. That's not true, Laura. This is who I really am, not some caricature of a superstar musician."

"But you didn't trust me, or that I could know that information and still have feelings for you..." she started.

"I barely knew you. When you're a celebrity, your guard has to be up or..."

"Or I might have wanted you for the money?" she said, her hands on her hips.

"That's not what I was saying at all. Look," he said, walking forward and grasping her hands, "I've never felt this way about a woman. I love you, Laura. I'm not going to deny it. But what I need to know is if you love me too? Can we work on getting past this?"

She looked away from him, tears building up in her eyes. "I don't know, Sawyer. I feel like I don't really know you. I've already been with one man who turned out to be someone else."

He dropped her hands and stiffened, his jaw tight. "No. You're right. We don't really know each other. I thought you were the one woman on Earth who wouldn't care about my fame, but it turns out you do. So maybe I should just take Dan's offer…" he said as he started walking away.

"Dan? What offer?" she called to him.

Sawyer turned one last time. "I'm going to go be what everyone thinks I should be. A freaking sell-out."

LAURA SAT at the kitchen table, drinking a cup of coffee and staring into space. She wanted to believe him. She wanted to just forget all of this had happened, but how could she? The last thing she needed in her life was another romantic drama to upend her whole world.

"You look exhausted, Laura. Is there anything I can do?" Addy asked as she sat down across from her. "Besides apologize again?"

Laura smiled sadly. "I'm not mad at you, Addy. I understand you were just protecting your friend."

"Did you talk to Sawyer?"

"Yes. A little while ago he found me on the beach."

"And did you guys work anything out?" Addy asked hopefully.

"No. I just don't understand why he couldn't trust me."

"Did he mention someone named Paula to you?"

"No. Who's Paula?" Laura asked, ready for some other huge secret to be revealed.

"I probably shouldn't break Sawyer's confidence here, but I'm going to because I know how much he cares about you, and I want to see y'all work this out."

"Okay…"

"Sawyer told me that a few years ago, after his second album, he met a woman named Paula at a Nashville coffee shop. At first, she was kind of a fangirl, but then they started getting close. He thought she really liked him for who he was. This was at the height of his career when he was playing the big stages, but what he really wanted was to be in love with a normal woman. She played that part for almost six months before one day he found out she'd been taking out credit in his name and using his debit card. He lost thousands of dollars and ended up in court with this woman. It broke him, Laura. He stopped trusting women. He didn't date anymore. So when you came along and truly had no idea who he was, it felt like his only real chance at being himself and finding a woman who might love him just because he was Sawyer."

Laura's eyes welled with tears. "I hate that someone did that to him."

"Look, you don't have to make a decision right now. But just don't give up on him altogether, sweetie. Sawyer is a good, good man. Hard to find someone like him, trust me. He would be loyal to you and protect you until his last breath. Don't throw that away without really thinking about it, okay?"

With that, Addy got up and went upstairs to tend to her young daughter, and Laura was left wondering if she'd ever have what Addy had. A man who loved her. A child who needed her. A simple, beautiful life.

～

IT HAD BEEN days since Laura had seen Sawyer anywhere around town. She was worried. After making amends with Addy, she decided to stay at the inn for awhile longer until she could find a place either in Savannah or January Cove. Everything just seemed so up in the air right now.

No one seemed to know where Sawyer was. Now that his leg had healed enough, he had been driving again, and Laura hadn't seen his car at home for days.

"I'll take one of everything!" Laura heard a woman's big booming voice say from behind her. When she turned around, she was so happy to see her aunt Dahlia standing there with a huge smile on her face.

"Aunt Dahlia! Oh my goodness! What a surprise. I didn't know you were coming!"

Her aunt scooped her into a big bear hug, and Laura struggled for her next breath. When she finally released her, Laura smiled.

"Well, honey, you're certainly a sight for sore eyes!" Dahlia said. "And look at this place! What a gorgeous shop you've got here, Laura. Your mother would be so proud of you."

The mention of her mother put butterflies in Laura's stomach. She missed her so much.

"I'm so glad you're here. I needed to see a familiar face," Laura said, forcing herself to look happy. Inside, she was missing Sawyer and wishing she had reacted differently and seen his side.

Dahlia looked around to make sure no other customers were in the store. "Yes. Carrie told me about your situation with a young man named Sawyer."

"She's a big mouth." Laura sat down on one of the bar stools and put her head in her hands. "I think I screwed up big time."

"She loves you."

"I know. But she's still a big mouth," Laura said with a chuckle. "Listen, I'm about to close up for the night. Why don't we head across the street, and you can stay with me at Addy's."

"Sweetie, I've already secured a room there. You know I'm organized to a fault!"

❧

LAURA SAT on the bed listening to Dahlia recount all of the "gossip" about her farm animals and some of their extended family members, but her mind was elsewhere. Had she done the wrong thing with Sawyer? And what did he mean about becoming a sell-out?

"Hello? Earth to Laura..." Dahlia said, waving her hand in front of Laura's face.

"I'm sorry. It's just been a very exhausting few days. So how was your trip out here?"

"Don't change the subject on me, missy. I know you better than that. You're a different person out here. More confident. Maybe even happier, except for the whole man trouble situation. Tell me about him."

"I don't want to talk about him, Aunt Dahlia." She stood and walked to the corner of the room, noticing her mother's vision board propped against the dresser. "He made me do things."

"What? What kind of things?" Dahlia asked, standing up with her hands on her rotund hips. Her long black skirt, that looked like it was made from paper and wheat mixed together, made rustling sounds from the force of her popping up off the bed.

"No. I don't mean it like that," Laura said. She turned to face her aunt. "I rode a rollercoaster. And a motorcycle."

"You? You've always been scared of your own

shadow." Dahlia's mouth was hanging open. "I didn't realize you ever wanted to do those things."

Laura smiled and picked up the board. "I didn't. I found my mother's vision board under her bed when I was cleaning out her house. Carrie convinced me to complete some of the items as a way of honoring my mother and starting over at the same time."

Dahlia reached out and took the board from Laura's hands. Her face had a look of shock, but also of recognition. "This was under her bed?"

"Yeah. Looked like it had been there for many years with the amount of dust piled on it. I was so surprised that my mother wanted to do any of those things. One of the places on the board was January Cove, so that's how I ended up here."

Dahlia took a deep breath. "So you did these things because your mother never got to?" She rubbed her fingers across the old paper and smiled.

"Yes. It made me feel closer to her. It made me feel alive again... Well, Sawyer made me feel alive again." She slumped down into an arm chair next to the bed.

"Laura, you know sometimes people just want to be accepted for who they really are. Maybe Sawyer handled it the wrong way, but for the right reasons."

"You're taking his side?"

Dahlia crossed the room and sat on the edge of the bed, her hand on Laura's knee. "Of course not. What I'm saying is that you're still raw from what

Ted did to you. You thought your husband was loyal, and he wasn't. He had a secret life you knew nothing about. But that's not what Sawyer did. Not really. He liked you so much that he wanted you to know the real him. The person inside. If you think about it, it really is sweet. He laid himself out there, raw."

Laura thought for a minute and realized her aunt was right. He had been kind and giving to her. He'd spent hours working for no pay. He'd taken her on adventures just to see her smile. He'd forgiven her when she hit him with her car.

"I really messed up. Ugh…" she said, putting her head in her hands. "And now I don't know where he is or what to do."

"Well, I'd start by asking around because I bet somebody knows where he is."

"You're right," Laura said, standing up.

"One more thing."

"Yes?" Laura said, turning to her aunt.

"Sometimes things aren't what they seem."

"True. But what does that have to do with this situation?"

"You shouldn't try to live someone else's dreams, honey."

"I know. Sawyer told me that too. I'm working on my own vision board. See?" She held up a piece of poster board that was propped behind the vanity.

"Good. Because this one… well, it's mine."

"What?"

"I created it many years ago, but I forgot to take it with me after a visit. I had gone to Baltimore for some self-help conference, you know, trying to better myself. They told us to create a vision board, so I did. These were *my* dreams, Laura, not your mother's. In fact, she laughed at most of them. Told me I was too adventurous for my own good."

"Oh my gosh… So I moved here for no reason?"

"Oh, I wouldn't say that. Looks like you've changed your whole life in a matter of weeks. You've got a thriving business. You met a wonderful man. You've met great friends. I think you just needed a little push."

"Can I ask you something? Why did you put a picture of January Cove on your board?" Laura asked before walking out of the room.

Dahlia laughed. "I cut it out of a travel magazine as a placeholder for wanting a beach house. I didn't know a darn thing about this place. Never been here in my life."

Laura rolled her eyes at the irony of it all and laughed. "I need to go do some damage control. Can you stay here until I get back?"

Dahlia nodded and Laura ran out the door, hopeful that someone could tell her where Sawyer had gone.

CHAPTER 13

The Lamont Theater was a happening place at night, and Laura struggled to find Brad. Addy had said her brother was sometimes there helping his girlfriend, Ronni, oversee the place.

She walked inside and looked around, but she mostly saw families and teenagers there for a good movie or maybe to ride the go-carts out back.

"Can I help you?" a teenage girl asked from behind the counter.

"Yes. I'm looking for... Brad!" Laura spotted him standing in the arcade, fiddling with something behind one of the machines.

"Laura! Welcome to the Lamont. What's up?"

"Can I talk to you for a second?" she asked. Brad nodded and waved her into the small office.

"Everything okay?" he asked, leaning against the desk.

197

"Do you happen to know where Sawyer went? I haven't seen him for days and..." She could tell by the look on his face that he knew something.

"Sawyer went back to Nashville, Laura."

"Oh no..." she said, sinking down into a cheap office chair.

"He was pretty upset when he left, but he gave me something for you."

"For me?"

"He told me that if you came looking for him, I should give it to you. Not sure what it is, but I have it here in my bag." He pulled a backpack from behind the desk and handed her a small gift bag that was sealed up with a ribbon. "Kind of girly, but here it is..."

"Well, I *am* a girl, Brad," she said with a forced smile. "Thanks."

"Hey, Laura?" Brad called to her as she walked toward the door.

"Yes?"

"He's a good guy. He didn't mean any harm. I've never seen him this tied up about a woman before, and sometimes we men do stupid stuff when we're afraid we're going to lose the woman of our dreams."

"Would Ronni agree with that?" she asked.

"Most definitely."

With that, Laura left the Lamont, eager to get back to the inn and find out what Sawyer had left her.

"WELL, WHAT IS IT?" Dahlia asked, as she sat beside Laura on the bed and waited for her to open the package.

"Can I get a little privacy?" Laura asked, smiling at her aunt.

Dahlia nodded and stood. "I'll be rocking in one of those beautiful chairs on the porch if you need me."

Laura took a deep breath and untied the ribbon. She looked down inside and saw two items - a piece of paper and a CD.

Dear Laura,

If you're reading this, then it means that I'm back in Nashville signing a contract for a new album and a tour. While that might sound great to anyone else, I'd rather be in January Cove smelling cupcake batter and teaching kids how to play guitar and ending every night holding you in my arms.

So why did I leave?

Because you deserve a fresh start without me passing you everyday on the streets. If I had stayed in January Cove, I couldn't have stayed away from you. Every ocean breeze reminded me of how your hair would tickle my face while we snuggled in the sand. Every person walking by with one of your cupcakes reminded me of early morning kissing sessions behind the counter of Sweetcakes.

When you love someone, you do what's best for them. If that means going back to the life I left so that you can start your life over, then I'd do it over and over again for you.

God, Laura, I wanted things to be different with us. I promise I was going to tell you the real story about me the same day you found out, but Carrie beat me to it. I was a chicken. I should've trusted you.

The CD included is a song I wrote for you. I wrote it after our adventure together at the amusement park. That's when knew how I felt about you. I hope you like it, and I hope that when you hear one of my songs on the radio, you'll think back to our time fondly.

I love you, Laura. Keep chasing your own dreams. You deserve it.

Sawyer

Laura choked back her tears as she pulled the CD from the bag. Hoping that her laptop actually had a CD slot, she ran across the room to dig it out of its bag. Thankfully, it did have a slot, so she slipped the CD in and waited to hear his voice.

The song started with the soft sounds of his guitar. It wasn't professionally produced, obviously, but hearing him sing again made her soul stir. She could listen to him all day and night and never hear another piece of classical music again.

As she listened to his words, her heart clenched at the thought of what she'd lost. He was singing about her - her strength, her beauty, her smile. As soon as the song ended, Laura bolted from the house again and went straight back to the Lamont.

"Brad!" she yelled as she ran through the doors. People were staring at her like she was an idiot or possibly a danger to society.

"Laura, hold it down, honey," Brad said with a painted-on smile as he ushered her into the office again. "What's wrong?"

"I need to find Sawyer. I need to stop him from signing that contract."

"Laura, he's been gone for days now. He's probably already signed it…"

"I have to find out. Please. Help me get to him."

"Why don't you just call him?"

"No. I need to see him. Do you know his address in Nashville?"

"You're going to drive to Nashville tonight?"

She thought for a moment. "Yes. I am."

A few minutes later, she had Sawyer's address in her hand. She rushed back to see her aunt and explain that she was going to be gone for a couple of days.

"I'm sorry, aunt Dahlia. I know you just got here…"

"Honey, it's fine. Love is love," she said with a wink. "I'll watch the store while your gone. It reminds me of my sandwich shop I used to run back in the old days."

She knew Dahlia would have no trouble running

the bakery. She was an exceptional baker herself and probably taught Sarah everything she knew.

"I love you," Laura said, hugging her aunt tightly. "I'll be back as soon as I can!"

Laura shoved a few things into a bag, and ran straight out the door for an almost eight hour drive to find the man of her dreams.

THE DRIVE to Nashville in the middle of the night had been tough. She was already tired from a long day at work, so keeping her eyes open while driving such a long distance had been difficult.

After stopping for coffee twice along the way, caffeine was her new best friend as she rolled into the heart of Nashville on fumes, both literally and figuratively. Her car needed gas, but she had to find Sawyer first. The sun had risen over the beautiful city, and her aim was to find the man she loved and tell him.

She pulled into the quaint neighborhood where Sawyer lived and started looking for his house. Her eyes were glazing over, and although she normally had great vision, the address in her hand was blurry from hours of driving.

"Forty-two thirteen… Wait. Is that right?" she said to herself as she looked at the street numbers and then back down at the paper. "Dang it. Is that a three…"

And then the sound she never wanted to hear again. A loud thump hit the front of her car as she came to an immediate stop, yet she saw nothing in front of her.

"Oh my God! Not again!" she said to herself as she flung open her door. As if in a scene from the movie Groundhog Day, she looked on the ground and saw Sawyer laying there. "Sawyer! Oh no! Are you hurt?"

"Jeez, woman, is your car just attracted to me or something?" he said. Thank goodness he was laughing. Apparently, she had only knocked him over this time.

"I'm so sorry! Are you okay?"

He smiled. "It depends."

"On what?" She continued checking him over, looking for any sign that she had hurt him again.

"On why you're here," he said softly, touching a strand of her hair with his fingers. "Let's get out of the road. This isn't January Cove."

She stood and held out a hand to him. He stood with her, brushing off his shorts.

"You have a scrape on your leg, Sawyer…"

He looked down and smiled back at her. "I'll live. Now, what on Earth are you doing here in Nashville? You look exhausted, Laura."

She stood there like a deer caught in the headlights for a moment and took a breath. "I haven't slept in over twenty-four hours."

"Let's sit down," he said, pointing to a park bench near the road. As they sat down, a man with a camera snapped a shot of them from the bushes. "Get out of here!" Sawyer yelled. The man laughed and then walked down the street. "Damn, paparazzi. They usually don't bug me too much around my house."

"He's probably wondering why I just mowed you down with my car," she said with a slight smile. "I can't imagine what pictures will be on the front of the tabloids this week."

"Let me park your car. We'll go inside and talk." He took her keys and moved her car to a more suitable spot. "It's this way."

She followed him into a sizable older home with white columns and a black wrought iron front gate. As they walked, she noticed he was wearing running clothes. She must have hit him during his morning exercise regimen.

"Coffee?" he asked as they walked into the kitchen.

"Please."

"So, tell me why you're here. Why did you drive all night?" he asked as he poured them both a cup.

"Because Brad gave me your gift," she said softly.

Sawyer stopped moving for a moment and then lifted both cups and carried them to the breakfast bar.

"I see. You didn't have to come, Laura. I know you don't want to be around me, and I've accepted that. I don't like it, but I want you to have your dream life."

"You *are* my dream life."

He looked at her, his eyes wide. "What?"

"It hurt me when you didn't tell me who you were, but I was wrong in the way I reacted. Seeing that guy out there snap a picture of you just proves your point. You didn't know if I would like you for your money or fame, and you just wanted to see if I would like you for you. I get it now."

"You get it now? Why didn't you get it back in January Cove, Laura?" he asked, clearly frustrated.

"Because it turns out everything isn't always as it seems."

"You're talking in riddles," he said, taking a sip of his coffee.

"That dream board wasn't my mother's. It was my wild and crazy aunt's."

Sawyer almost spit his coffee out, stifling a laugh that was battling to come out. "Seriously? Oh my gosh, that's funny."

She stood and walked around the counter, taking Sawyer's coffee from his hands and setting it on the countertop. She took his hands in hers and stared up into his eyes.

"I'm tired of living everyone else's dreams, Sawyer. I want to live my dreams. And the only person I want to do that with is you. Being with you changed me. You make me want to take chances."

"What are you saying, Laura?"

"I'm saying that I love you, and I will stay here in Nashville with you if I have to. I know you signed that new contract, and I'm sorry that you felt you had to do it because of me. But as soon as it's up, I want you to come back to January Cove with me. Because you deserve to live your dreams, no matter how big or small."

"You love me?" he asked with a smile, as if that was the only part he heard.

"I do."

"Well, I love you too, Laura Bennett. Even if you do keep hitting me with your car. Seriously, stop doing that." His dimpled smile gave her chills up and down her spine. He pulled her into his chest and kissed the top of her head. "But you can't stay in Nashville."

"What? Why?"

"Because Sweetcakes is in January Cove. That's your baby."

"You're my baby," she whispered as she rose up on her tip toes and lightly kissed him.

"And I love to hear that..." he said before deepening their kiss. "But I won't be here."

Laura pulled back. "Your tour is already starting? I don't know much about the music business, but don't you have to record the album first?"

Sawyer smiled. "I didn't sign the contract, Laura. I just couldn't do it."

"So what have you been doing here all this time?" she asked.

"Waiting for you. And praying that you would show up on my doorstep."

She grinned and jumped up into his arms, her legs coiled tightly around his waist. "Thank God! So we can go home? Back to January Cove?"

"Yes, we can go home," he said, pulling her to him tightly before setting her up on the kitchen counter in front of him. "Of course, you'll need a night to rest before we leave, and I just happen to have a bedroom right here in this house..."

Laura smiled brightly. "Who needs a bedroom when I can *rest* right here on this kitchen island?"

"I do like the way you think, Laura Bennett."

"WE SOLD OVER ONE-HUNDRED CUPCAKES TODAY!" Katie said with her big, brace-covered smile. The teenager had been working with Laura for just a few weeks, but she was a hard worker and good with the customers.

"That's awesome! Thanks for your help today. You'll be a manager in no time," Laura said with a wink, patting Katie on the back as the young girl went out the front door.

Sawyer walked in just as she was closing up and swept Laura into hug. He nuzzled his nose against her hair and sucked in a sharp breath.

"Today's special was banana pudding cupcakes?"

"How do you do that?" she asked with a laugh.

"I have very keen senses, Miss Bennett. For instance, my sense of smell is nothing compared to my sense of taste," he said, bending down and stealing a long, slow kiss. "You had a vanilla latte from Jolt?"

"And you had garlic pasta from Zach's?"

Sawyer pulled back and laughed, covering his mouth with his hand. "Sorry. I ran out of gum."

"So how was your day?" she asked as she slipped her arms around his waist again.

"Great. Tommy actually learned that new chord I was showing him on the guitar. We're planning to have a whole talent show at the end of camp next week, and I can't wait for you to see the progress these kids have made. I'm so proud of them."

"Well, I'm proud of you, Sawyer." She kissed him lightly on his neck and then made her way to his lips again.

"You are? Really? Even though I'm not a big superstar anymore?"

"You're my superstar, Sawyer Griffin, and that's all that counts."

~

FIND a list of all of Rachel Hanna's books at www. RachelHannaAuthor.com.

Copyright © 2016 by Rachel Hanna

All rights reserved.

No part of this book may be reproduced in any form or by any electronic or mechanical means, including information storage and retrieval systems, without written permission from the author, except for the use of brief quotations in a book review.

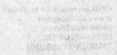

CPSIA information can be obtained
at www.ICGtesting.com
Printed in the USA
LVHW041924280122
709583LV00015B/2204